FULL COLOR

VINNI GEORGE

Full Color

Cover Design: Alison Millsaps, Ozark Witch Cover Design

Editing: Angela O'Connell

Proofreading: Lori Parks

First Edition

March 2025

ABOUT THIS BOOK

Quin Hunter likes the quiet life. He runs his gallery, forges famous art, and operates a fence where black-market buyers get fakes and the real pieces get returned to their rightful owners. Nice and simple. He doesn't do fieldwork. But a call from his twin thrusts him into the action, and now he and his brothers are racing the clock to steal a painting from someone who never should have had it in the first place.

Dimitri Crysanthos is no stranger to mistakes. All he wanted to do was make life easier for his sister. Instead, he ended up making everything harder for both of them. With his life and his sister's hanging in the balance, he has no choice but to do whatever one of the most ruthless men in Amsterdam tells him to do. All Dimitri wants is to stay alive...until a stranger changes everything. Now Dimitri craves something terrifying, something that will put him and his sister in even more danger—his freedom.

The stakes of the heist have changed, and Quin refuses to quit until Dimitri is safe for good. Can the ORCA team get the art and Quin's fated mate out of Amsterdam, or are the odds too stacked against them?

Full Color is book three in the Organization for the Return of Criminals and Assets (ORCA) series, featuring an orca shifter art forger who isn't keen on fieldwork, a chameleon shifter with a lucrative secret talent, and a heist where the target is far more valuable than a stolen painting!

CHAPTER ONE

QUIN

"QUIN, we found the painting. You need to get to Amsterdam." Cal's words rang in my ears as I tried to get my thoughts together. He'd found *The Evolution of Man,* which meant only one question remained.

"Is it the original or a forgery?"

My twin huffed on the other end of the line. "I have no fucking clue. That's why you need to get to Amsterdam, like now."

Even from half a world away and with the weird static in our twin bond, I could sense there was something important Cal wasn't telling me, but without being able to see him and read his expression, there was no easy way to ferret it out. Which was immensely frustrating.

But that was Cal—the walking embodiment of immense frustration.

And now he was asking me to walk into a situation blind, which was honestly much more his thing than it had ever been mine.

I pinched the bridge of my nose and sat in the unoccupied leather club chair in front of the unlit fireplace in my study. Our older brother, Nero, sat in the other club chair, a snifter of my favorite cognac clutched in his hand. The delicate glass looked ridiculous in his huge paw, but he'd taken a liking to the top-shelf spirits I preferred after I'd generously shared some of my coveted Pappy Van Winkle as a way to calm him down after his mate, Felix, had been kidnapped. Nero had been systematically sampling his way through my extensive collection of exclusive and expensive single-barrel bourbons, whiskeys, and cognacs since. To say I'd created a monster was an understatement.

"What's going on?" He gestured at the phone, and I pulled it away from my ear, hitting the speaker button and setting it on the small, antique mahogany table between us.

Cal's voice filled the space. "Why am I on speaker?"

I sighed, but I didn't think he could hear it. "Nero's here. It makes sense for you to tell both of us what's going on."

"Hi, Cal." It had been my twin's fault Felix had been kidnapped, and while Nero had forgiven him, mostly, there was still a little tension there.

"Uh, hey. Everything good?" To my ears, Cal's voice lacked some of its usual bravado, but Nero didn't seem to notice.

Nero nodded. "Business as usual here. What's happening there?"

"Jack and I found the painting, but we can't tell if it's a fake. We need Quin here ASAP."

"Who has it?" Nero took a small drink from his snifter, and I bit the inside of my cheek to keep from smiling. My older brother had taken my request to sip the expensive spirits instead of chugging them like a Neanderthal seriously. I might be able to make a gentleman out of him after all.

"Stefan Dasselaar. He's hosting a gala next week. From what we could find out, it looks like he's planning to auction off multiple stolen art pieces, and he's been teasing something big. We found out tonight that it's the painting."

Nero set the snifter down and rubbed his hands together. "What are you thinking?"

"I think we need to be holding more of the cards."

A wash of anticipation that wasn't mine pulsed through my body. My twin bond with Cal had been shaky for a while, more so since he'd found and claimed his fated mate in his former rival, great white shark shifter, Jack Grayson, but the odd giddiness I felt from his end of our bond meant only one thing.

"You think we should steal the painting before Dasselaar can auction it to the highest bidder."

Nero's eyebrow rose as Cal confirmed. "Bingo. Got it in one, Quinny."

I rolled my eyes at his use of the annoying nickname, but I didn't understand what having the painting would do for us except paint a bigger target on our backs. "I know I'm not the art thief"—I nodded at Nero—"or the field operative here, but why do we want the painting? Doesn't the fact that Dasselaar has it prove he's behind Felix's kidnapping and the threats on his life?"

My older brother picked up the little snifter again and rolled it between his large palms, his face twisted up in thought. It was a long moment before he spoke again. "No. If Dasselaar had the painting, or at least knew where it was so he could have a crew steal it, he would have had no reason to go after Felix or the FBI file Felix hacked. Whoever is after the information Felix has is looking for leads on who has the painting because they don't know."

"But have they figured out Dasselaar has it?" Cal's question hung in the air.

Nero shook his head. "I think we have to assume if we figured it out, someone else has too, or they will after the gala, which means we need to assume someone else is going to try to make a play for the painting."

"According to Reuben, there are too many people on that list, but my money is on anyone who has a vested interest in the painting being at Dasselaar's gala if for no other reason than to find out if the big score Dasselaar is teasing is *The Evolution of Man*." That was Jack's voice.

"Hey, Jack." Nero leaned toward the phone.

"Hey. I'm on the other line with Reuben, so I'll be in and out."

"Sounds good."

Jack laughed without humor. "Maybe not. Feels like shit's gotten real complicated."

Cal grumbled something in the background, then the unmistakable sounds of kissing came over the line. I looked away from where the phone sat on the table like I was trying to give them privacy. I was happy for Cal and Jack. I really was. But my stomach still twisted with jealousy over what they had that I had yet to find.

Picking up the snifter of cognac I'd poured myself, I knocked it back in one gulp, the burn a pleasant distraction from the hollow feeling in my chest. Nero raised an eyebrow in my direction, but I shook my head, standing to pour myself more.

"Can we get back to this please?" Nero asked, and clothes rustled from Jack and Cal's end of the line."

"Uh, sorry. Newly mated. You know how it is." Cal sounded unrepentant, and Nero's smirk said he did, in fact, understand.

I wished I did.

"We need a way into that gala." Nero drummed his fingers on the armrest of his chair. "Any chance Reuben can work some magic?"

I didn't hear Jack's reply as I moved behind my desk and started sifting through the papers I had there, looking for the blood-red envelope I'd come across a few days ago. It peeked out from a stack of inventory and sales reports, and I yanked it out of the pile. Cal, Jack, and Nero continued to talk while I slid the single sheet of heavy cream cardstock out of the envelope addressed to our grandmother and scanned the gold-embossed text.

"We technically have an invitation, as in we have one in our possession." I held up the invitation and crossed the room, returning to where Nero was still seated, now staring at me.

"What do you mean?" Nero asked. I'd forgotten I'd told everyone else, including Cal and Jack, about the invitation our grandmother had received at my gallery, but I hadn't mentioned it to Nero. Lowering into my previously vacated seat, I passed the sheet of expensive cardstock to Nero.

"Dasselaar invited Juno to the gala."

"Bastard's cocky as fuck." Cal wasn't wrong.

Nero sat back in his chair, the invitation held between

two of his thick fingers as he studied it. "It's definitely ballsy as hell to invite a thief known to want the painting to the gala where you're allegedly going to auction it off. I think we need to proceed with caution. Dasselaar is clearly working some sort of angle. If he invited Juno, I think we're correct in assuming he invited anyone and everyone he can think of who has a vested interest in the painting."

Swirling the new measure of cognac in my glass, I nodded. "I agree. It makes the most sense in terms of maximizing his profit on the piece. If he puts it up for auction to bidders who've spent their lives attempting to steal it against bidders who have ridiculous sums of money to play with, it's going to drive the bidding through the roof and net Dasselaar a mountain of money. That's just good business. It's exactly what I would do. Plus, it's obviously a giant middle finger to everyone who couldn't manage to steal it. Juno included."

Nero smiled at me, a glimmer of something that looked remarkably like pride in his eyes before he turned his attention back to the phone. "If it's the real painting. Even if it's not, once word gets out that Dasselaar has the painting, thieves are going to come crawling out of the woodwork. He's got to know that, so his security is going to be tighter than tight."

Cal and Jack had a conversation away from the phone before Cal's voice came over the line again. "Jack was able to hack his computer at the gallery, including his encrypted emails, and it looks like he's already planning to increase security at the gallery while the painting is there."

"Keep an eye on his setup. We need to know as much as we can before we decide if it's worth trying to steal it from

Dasselaar or if we're better off waiting until the painting changes hands." Nero, who'd been absently tapping the invitation on the edge of the table, passed it back to me. "If the invitation was addressed to Juno, how are we going to get into the gala? Should I have Julius try to contact her again?"

"I have a plan for that too. Juno's invitation is our backup plan, but I think we need to try to score our own invitation."

Nero narrowed his eyes. "Explain."

"I have a contact in Amsterdam who does a lot of business in the US. His base of operations in the States is in San Francisco, but he's looking to move stolen art up the coast and out through Vancouver. We've been trying to organize a meeting, but the timing has never worked out. When you asked Felix and Julius to dig up whatever they could find on Dasselaar, I learned my contact is one of Dasselaar's associates."

"So what's your plan?" Jack asked.

"We all know the art world is a small one. I'm going to reach out and let my contact know I'll be in Amsterdam. When I get the meeting, I'll plant some seeds letting him know I'm interested in connecting with more European contacts, that I'm looking to expand my client list. I've worked hard to build a reputation that I'm incredibly selective in whom I choose to work with. If it comes out that I'm taking on new clients, there should be interest in helping to make those connections. Besides, Dasselaar already knows I'm connected to Juno since he sent her invitation to my gallery."

"I like it." Cal sounded impressed. "Nero, what do you think?"

Our older brother nodded. "I think it feels like a long shot, but I trust you, Quin. If you think you can get on this guest list by working your contacts, I'm willing to try it. What do you need from us?"

I shrugged. "Obviously, I need to get to Amsterdam. The sooner the better. I'll reach out to my contact now and let him know I'm coming to him. Dasselaar's gala is a big deal. There's no way he won't be in town for it."

"So what do we do about Juno's invitation?" Nero handed the paper back to me.

"I think we ignore it for now. Pretend we don't know Dasselaar invited her."

Jack made an approving noise. "Is it going to be too much of a coincidence if you show up in Amsterdam at the same time as Dasselaar's gala when Juno's invitation was sent to your gallery?"

Nero shrugged. "Would Dasselaar assume we're going to open her mail? Wouldn't Quin just pass it along to her?"

"I don't know, but I think Quin's right. We need to get our own invitation. Playing dumb about Juno's invite works for now." I could tell from his tone that Cal was working through the beginnings of our plan and trying to connect the dots. Unfortunately, we didn't have enough information for the dots to form any sort of clear picture. But I had a gut feeling as soon as I got to Amsterdam, things would start to come together.

Nero leaned back in his chair. "I'll call Hadrian and see if he's got a way to get us to Amsterdam fast."

"Reuben has a plane at Sea-Tac, but he doesn't have a

pilot." Jack's voice sounded like it was coming from far away from the phone. "If your cousin can fly it, Reuben says you're welcome to use it."

"Hade can fly it. I'll make the call. Tell Reuben we'll take him up on his offer." Nero pushed out of his chair and slid his cell phone from his pocket.

"Good. Jack and I will keep an eye on things here. We'll talk to Reuben about getting a bigger place that we can use as a base of operations. For now, we have a hotel suite. Meet us here unless we can get something together sooner. We'll let you know."

"I'll get in touch with my contact."

"Excellent. Rally the troops, since I assume Julius and Felix aren't going to let you come to Amsterdam without them, and we'll keep you posted."

Nero nodded, and Cal and Jack disconnected the call. I looked down at the heavy cardstock in my hand. I hoped I hadn't promised my brothers more than I could deliver. It was a new feeling for me to be part of their team, and I didn't want to screw it up. Not that I thought I would.

Nero's hand on my shoulder made me glance up. "You okay?"

Sliding into the persona I used when I sat across the table from the criminals on my client list, I gave my brother my best unaffected half smile. "I'm fine. Just trying to compute the time difference between here and Amsterdam. I want an answer about the meeting before we get on the plane."

Nero smiled, the thrill of the hunt flashing in his eyes, and clapped me on the shoulder. "I'm going to go brief

Julius and Felix and call Hade. Make sure you pack your tux."

"Which one?"

My brother laughed. "You might be the only person I know who owns multiple tuxes. Might as well pack them all."

When he was gone, the door to my study clicking shut behind him, I slid into my desk chair and pulled out my laptop. Julius had set it up so it was completely secure, and I pulled up the encrypted email program I used to correspond with my clients. Niels Zwart was a weasel shifter—appropriate given his line of work procuring and selling stolen goods. So far, I'd never met him, but he'd received my contact information via a recommendation from one of his colleagues. We'd tried to set up a meeting when he was in the States last spring, but he'd had to cancel his trip at the last minute, and I'd been unable to make it to Amsterdam at the time.

Funny how things worked out sometimes.

I reopened our email thread and told him I'd be in Amsterdam on business for the next several days and had some available time if he was free. Once the email was sent, I rocked back in my chair and closed my eyes.

I was damn good at running my gallery and selecting my clients. I'd had countless meetings with criminal kingpins from around the globe, but something about this meeting felt more important. Maybe it was because my brothers were counting on me, and I'd never been in that position before. Usually, I was an island, only working with Julius to make sure the payments for my services were received into the correct accounts.

But now I had a valuable role to play.

A role that would bring us one step closer to finding out who was behind the attempt on Felix's life and his kidnapping. I knew in my gut that this was bigger than we thought. Someone was pulling the strings, and I hoped we wouldn't get tangled up in them.

Maybe we already were.

Pushing away from my desk, I closed my laptop and tucked it under my arm. Time to pack.

My phone buzzed in my pocket before I was halfway up the stairs.

The meeting with Zwart was set.

CHAPTER TWO

DIMITRI

"FUCK!" I sat up quickly, my heart racing from the nightmare, and hands shaking, I reached blindly for the lamp on the bedside table. It took me three attempts to turn on the light, but when the warm glow of the single bulb illuminated the space, my pulse finally began to slow.

As much as it ever did within the gilded walls of my prison.

My suite in Stefan Dasselaar's estate was on the smaller side, but it was comfortable. I had a large bed, an en suite bathroom, and a wardrobe full of clothes I didn't own that I was meant to wear so I didn't embarrass Dasselaar when he trotted me out to entertain his friends and reassure his investors that they were buying only the finest stolen merchandise.

For a while, I'd thought the price I was paying to keep my sister safe was worth it. Things could certainly have been worse. The threat of Dasselaar backing out of our deal always hung over my head, but while I was useful to him, he'd keep me around.

Until three nights ago.

Until he killed an innocent man right in front of me.

Until I watched blood seep from the bullet hole in the truck driver's chest and spread out in dark garnet rivers from under his lifeless body.

Even now, days later, my nose burned with the acrid scent of the gunshot and the metallic tang of blood. So much blood.

My stomach turned over, and I swallowed down the bile rising in my throat.

I knew now that any safety I thought I had as Dasselaar's little toy had always been an illusion. The truck driver had been innocent, merely a man who'd taken an extra job delivering to the gallery after hours, and he'd paid for that choice with his life.

All because that ill-fated decision meant he knew more about Dasselaar and his dealings than he should.

I had been Dasselaar's prisoner, his property, for over a year. I'd met hundreds of his clients and seen millions of dollars of stolen property pass through his gallery and the estate. If that truck driver was a liability, what was I?

A dead man walking.

A man who'd been on borrowed time since the day I'd met Stefan Dasselaar.

But maybe I'd known that since the day I'd tried to sell him a piece of forged art. I hadn't known who he really was then. I'd thought he was just a gallery owner like the hundreds of others in Amsterdam, and I was just trying to make sure my sister had the resources she needed to finish art school and stay healthy.

Then I'd found him in our tiny apartment, his huge

frame dominating the space as he perched on the edge of our tiny secondhand sofa, lying in wait, a predator stalking his prey. It was a small miracle that I'd been the one to get home first. I wasn't sure what would have happened to my sister if she'd been the first to arrive back at our apartment. It made me nauseous to even think about it.

Dasselaar was there because he had discovered my deception and wanted to know how I'd been able to accomplish the nearly perfect forgery. When I'd refused to explain, attempting to lie, saying I had no idea it was a fake, Dasselaar had recited every detail of my life, the threat to me and my sister barely veiled within his words. He could get her kicked out of school, both of us thrown out of Amsterdam, and Athina blacklisted from every art school in Europe. He knew we were in Amsterdam illegally, without visas, and lacking permission from the Cypriot government to leave Cyprus. He knew our parents were both dead, having succumbed to the same rare disease Athina had. Dasselaar knew we had forged the documents we needed to get out of Cyprus and to get Athina into school. And worst of all, he knew we were chameleon shifters.

That was the moment I realized the gravity of my mistake.

Stefan Dasselaar was dangerous, and I had picked the wrong mark.

I should have stuck to selling art on the street, but the money tourists paid for paintings of bridges and bicycles barely kept the lights on, and since we were in Amsterdam illegally, we had no choice but to pay for Athina's medications through a shifter doctor who looked the other way when it came to things like enrollment in the Dutch health-care system.

Backed into a corner, I was forced to reveal my talent to Dasselaar—though now it felt like a curse—and Dasselaar had made me an offer I was in no position to refuse. In exchange for him not killing me for trying to deceive him or having my sister kicked out of the Netherlands, I would work for him. He would create a scholarship that funded my sister's education and paid all her living expenses, including the costs of her medications.

Which sounded great.

But of course, there was a catch.

I would be completely under Dasselaar's thumb, which meant I would be living in his house, never far from his sight, and I could only see my sister under direct supervision from Dasselaar or one of his musclebound goons.

Which is how Dasselaar's estate became my pretty cage.

I was no longer free, and now I knew I was little more than a liability.

Killing the truck driver in front of me was meant to send a message, and I'd heard it loud and clear.

My days were numbered.

I should have known the only way out of this situation would end with me in a body bag…or tossed into a shipping crate like the truck driver.

Another shudder rolled down my spine, but the terror that now wrapped around my heart, staining it black, would not abate. The only solace I had was that I knew how I would die. It was the question of when that continued to plague me.

In the few days since the bloody incident at the gallery,

only one thing had successfully driven back the nightmares. Pulling open the drawer in my nightstand, I extracted the single luxury Dasselaar allowed me to have as my own—a sketchbook and simple set of drawing pencils.

Flipping through the pages, I studied the image I'd drawn over and over again. My first sketches were of the man as he had been in Dasselaar's gallery, taking in the Renoir Dasselaar had made me prove was an original. I hadn't noticed at the time, but the man's posture as he considered the painting had been off, like it was not a pose he affected often. The lines of his broad shoulders were too tight, and his whole body was too stiff. But still, there was something deeply appealing about him, even if I knew for certain he was not an avid art collector as he had claimed. I would also bet my already forfeited life that his real name was not Calvin Smith.

My subsequent drawings had focused on his face, on the kindness in his eyes when they met mine over the forged Vermeer, on the anger that flashed through the rich umber depths when Dasselaar shoved me away. I'd seen those eyes in my dreams as often as I heard the gunshot in my nightmares, both haunting me in different ways.

In my early sketches, I'd drawn the man's eyes as they lived in my memory, but over time, the finer details began to change. The scar that marred the stranger's left eyebrow disappeared, and his facial hair gave way to a smooth, clean-shaven jaw. The black skin on the man's neck, which had been mostly hidden by his shirt, morphed into a bold vee of black that looked like a thick brushstroke. The lines of his body lost some of their bulk until the man on the page looked only vaguely familiar but achingly perfect.

The two men—the one from the gallery and the one comfortably tucked into the pages of my sketchbook—could have been brothers, but they were not the same. Still, something in me reached out to the man on the page like he was someone real, someone meant for me. Perhaps I had been caged for too long, my mind giving way to madness that could only be satisfied by a fictional prince who looked like someone I'd met once for too short a time.

In my heart, I wanted the stranger who stared up at me from my drawings to be real so badly. I wanted to believe he was the one who could set me free, and as dangerous as those dreams were, I let myself sink into them as I put pencil to paper and sketched him again, this time wrapped in the cool white sheets next to me, his dark brown eyes closed in sleep, his thick inky eyelashes casting shadows on his cheeks. In my mind, we had made love. He'd filled me until my body and my heart couldn't take more, and then he'd held me in his arms, the safety and security he offered more comforting than any blanket. The quiet moments that followed had woven us together so wherever he was, I was there too. The image in my mind and on the page were so real that I stretched out a hand to feel him, only to be met with cold where there should have been heat.

Like always, I was alone, trapped in a cell of my own making, with only the vaguest fantasy of freedom to keep me company. Tucking my sketchbook to my chest, I slipped lower under the covers, leaving the bedside lamp on as I willed myself to go back to sleep, praying it would be dreamless, knowing that either the nightmares that had plagued me or the sweet dream of my fictional lover's arms would leave a wound on my soul I had no hope of repairing.

But I'd never been lucky, and the scent of gunfire and rivers of crimson blood followed me into the morning, when two of Dasselaar's musclebound goons barged into my room to administer my daily dose of the antitransmutative drug Dasselaar used to keep me even further under this thumb. With the drug in my veins, I could shift enough to use my talents on Dasselaar's behalf, but I couldn't take my full chameleon form. Dasselaar was arrogant, but he wasn't stupid, and keeping me drugged ensured I couldn't slip through his hold.

The needle stabbed into my flesh, and I was certain of only one thing.

No one was coming to rescue me.

CHAPTER THREE

QUIN

NIELS ZWART SAT across from me in the dimly lit dim sum restaurant in Zeedijk, Amsterdam's Chinatown. The unassuming restaurant had been his choice, and as the late lunch crowd surrounded us, I understood why. We were hiding in plain sight, anonymous in the busy restaurant where everyone was focused on their own meal. Loud conversations around us masked anything we said to each other, and looking around, I also doubted we were the only table conducting borderline illegal business.

The restaurant wouldn't have been one I would have picked. I would have opted for a secluded table at a Michelin-starred establishment, but Zwart's choice worked too.

The faux leather chair creaked under me as I leaned back and studied the man across the table. He wore a designer suit, but unlike my own, which had been expertly tailored to fit me perfectly, Zwart's suit hung from his thin shoulders. He was short, his frame wiry. Auburn hair flecked with gray was swept back off his face and held in place with too much gel for my taste. His facial features were sharp, and his small, dark eyes darted around the room before they settled on me. He had thin lips, the top one bracketed by a skinny mustache. He had long fingers that were never still. Over the ten minutes we'd been seated at the table he'd shredded a paper napkin then twisted and braided the paper into a coil. If I didn't know better, I'd assume it was a sign of nerves, but Zwart's hands didn't shake. Even if I hadn't known ahead of our meeting that he was a weasel shifter, I would have been able to guess within seconds.

He'd refused to talk business until we'd ordered lunch, and as the first bamboo steamers filled with dumplings arrived at our table, he leaned over his plate and spoke.

"As you already know, I have special merchandise I need to move within the US. I've heard you are the man to contact to make sure my shipments arrive to my buyers efficiently."

Unfolding one of the paper napkins, I set it on my lap—manners were never out of style regardless of the environment—and selected a set of cheap wooden chopsticks from the chipped, red, plastic cup on the table. "If the merchandise you're looking to move is art, then yes, I'm the best."

Zwart smiled, his beady eyes bright. "Excellent. I have three pieces I've recently acquired. I'm selling one to a contact in Vancouver and the other two need to get from San Francisco to me here in Amsterdam." He reached into his pocket and pulled out several folded sheets of paper, sliding them across the table to me.

The pieces he needed moved were nowhere near the highest value items I'd passed through my gallery, but they were certainly hot. I recognized one of the pieces as one that had been stolen from a private collection in Los Angeles a little over half a year ago. According to my intel, it had been an inside job, which made me wonder how Zwart had come to acquire it, but those details were inconsequential to the matter at hand.

"Which piece is going to the Canadian buyer?"

Zwart had stuffed a dumpling into his mouth, and he pushed it into his cheek to answer. I did my best not to cringe. "The third one."

Perfect. The Roy Lichtenstein was the easiest for me to forge and the easiest for me to move. And I already had the forgery ready. Nero might have learned how to steal paintings at Juno's knee, but she taught me how to watch art and how it moved through the criminal underworld. The second I'd learned the Lichtenstein had been stolen, I had a feeling it would be only a matter of time before it ended up on my doorstep.

So I'd prepared accordingly.

Modern oil and acrylic—even if they are a specialized formula from the 1960s—on canvas is generally the easiest to reproduce since I didn't have to spend time making pigment-based oil paints using formulations from the eighteenth or nineteenth century. That's not to say I couldn't do it, and do it exceptionally well, it just wasn't as easy. If you knew where to source the right materials, it was easy to find contemporary acrylics that were impossible to discern from those used from the 1960s to the present. The Lichtenstein was a slam dunk and, honestly, a stroke of good luck.

I studied the painting on the sheet Zwart had given me for an extra second, not that I needed it since I knew every intimate detail of every single brush stroke on the canvas. "Who is your buyer?"

"Jean-Paul Bouchard."

I bit back the smile that threatened to creep across my lips. I'd done business with the lumber tycoon turned Canadian mafia don, known in certain circles as the Axeman, before, and we already had an excellent rapport.

"Have you already negotiated a price?"

Zwart swallowed the bite he'd been chewing as he watched my face for a reaction and shook his head. "Not yet. I just know he's interested in acquiring it."

"What were you hoping to get out of the painting?"

"Five million?" The question mark at the end of what should have been a statement told me everything Zwart's taste in restaurants hadn't disclosed. He knew nothing about the merchandise he held, which made this even easier for me.

"This is a Roy Lichtenstein."

Zwart shoved another dumpling in his mouth. "Okay."

Smoothing the napkin on my lap, I folded my hands over my knee. "In 2017, a Lichtenstein piece sold for one hundred sixty-five million dollars in a private sale."

The bombshell had the intended effect. Zwart began to choke, his face turning a disturbing shade of puce. Within seconds, one of the dark-suited men who'd been seated by the door stood and approached the table, but Zwart waved him away, reaching for his glass of water and downing half.

His voice was half an octave higher when he spoke again. "One hundred sixty-five million dollars? US dollars?"

I smiled. "Yes, US dollars." Picking up my chopsticks, I

selected a dumpling and bit into it, letting Zwart process the information I'd delivered. I had to admit, what the restaurant lacked in ambiance, it made up for in quality. The dumplings were delicious.

Zwart stared at me, waiting anxiously for me to elaborate, but I let the moment hold. It was all part of the game. He was on the hook, and I had every intention of letting him hang there for a moment. When I was finished with my dumpling and I'd demurely wiped my mouth, I continued. "That's not to say this particular piece is worth that amount. Unfortunately, it's not. But we can certainly do better than five."

"What are you thinking?"

"Twenty-five. Minimum."

Zwart's little eyes went comically wide. "Twen—twenty-five."

"At least."

My mark's face hardened. "I don't believe you."

I resisted the urge to roll my eyes and pulled my phone from my breast pocket. The screen showed several notifications from my brothers, but I ignored them. Making a show of glancing at my watch, I pulled up my contacts and tapped the screen. The lumber business started early, and it was already five thirty in Vancouver.

The call connected on the second ring.

"Quin Hunter. To what do I owe the pleasure?" A saw hummed in the background.

"Good morning, JP. I hope I'm not catching you at a bad time."

"Not at all. Had some business we had to take care of early this morning, but it's almost wrapped up." I knew that was code for something, or rather someone, taking a trip through the wood chipper, so I changed the subject.

"I understand you and I have a mutual colleague."

He laughed, the sound booming and deep. "I'm sure we have many mutual contacts. Who do you mean specifically?"

"Niels Zwart." Zwart visibly puffed up when I mentioned his name.

"Ah, yes. He has a piece I'm looking to acquire for my daughter as a wedding present."

"Congratulations. I wasn't aware Arlette was engaged."

"Wedding is next month." There was pride in his voice, and he'd given me several valuable pieces of information.

"Zwart has asked me to help him negotiate a price. Do you have time to do that now, or would you prefer to set up a call later today or this week?"

"We're both very busy, and you already have me on the line. How much is this going to cost me?"

"Thirty-five million."

Bouchard laughed again, this time without humor. "Quin, please. We've been doing business together for a long time. I know you can do better than that."

I could, and I would, but I went through the motions of explaining the value and rarity of the piece anyway.

Bouchard was quiet for a moment. "I can do fifteen."

I shook my head. "For fifteen, you're not getting it in time for the wedding. It will rot in customs for months. Thirty."

"Do you know how much this wedding is already costing me? Twenty."

"I can't get it out of customs in the timeframe you need

for less than twenty-five, and you know it. That's basically bargain basement for this piece. You're putting my reputation on the line. If you don't want it, I could suggest Zwart put it up for auction."

Bouchard sighed. "I hate doing business with you, Quin, but fine. I'm in at twenty-five. Zwart is damn lucky to have you."

"I just want Arlette to have the piece she wants for her special day."

"Fuck off. Send me the wire details."

"You know the deal. Half with the signed standard contract. The remainder on delivery."

"Yeah, yeah. You'll have the contract and the money today. If you ever feel like negotiating lumber prices, you call me."

I laughed, the thrill of victory thrumming in my veins. "You couldn't afford me."

"Tell me something I don't already know." The call disconnected.

Zwart studied me. "He went for it?"

"Twenty-five million. And since this is our first transaction, I'm willing to drop my usual seven percent fee to five percent."

Zwart opened his mouth, no doubt to negotiate, but I held up my hand. "My fee is not up for negotiation. If you don't like five percent, I'm happy to keep my standard seven."

He shook his head. "No. Five is more than reasonable."

"I thought so." I selected another dumpling and ate it carefully. "We'll need to talk logistics in a moment, but I'd be willing to extend the same five percent terms to any other contacts you can introduce me to while I'm here. And what I mean by that is, I'm willing to take six percent and cut you in on the other one percent."

Zwart's beady eyes went wide again, dollar signs flashing in them. He leaned forward like what he was about to tell me needed to be for my ears only. "Do you know Stefan Dasselaar?"

I pretended to think. "The name is familiar."

"He owns a gallery here, but we are all in a similar business. I have a feeling he would very much like to meet you, and I know for a fact that a number of parties who would be very interested in your services will be attending a gala he's hosting."

Sitting back in my chair again, I smoothed my napkin on my lap. "Those are connections I'd be interested in making."

Zwart nodded. "And you'd cut me in on any deals you close with contacts from the gala?"

"Absolutely."

He tried not to let it show, but there was greedy glee in his eyes. "Let me make a call." Pulling out his phone, he tapped the screen, then held the phone to his ear. When his contact on the other end, presumably Dasselaar, picked up, they had a short conversation in rapid Dutch, then Zwart ended the call and put his phone back in his pocket. "I gave Dasselaar your contact information. If he's interested, he'll be in touch."

"Thank you. I appreciate that. I think this could be very lucrative for both of us."

Zwart lifted his water glass in a toast. "Indeed."

An hour and a half later, my phone rang as Hadrian—

who had decided to stay in Amsterdam and act as my driver and bodyguard—and I returned to the royal penthouse suite Reuben had arranged for us to use as a base of operations. I had no idea why he'd decided to bankroll this mission, but I wasn't going to complain.

The number on the screen had a Dutch country code, and I smiled as I connected the call. "Quin Hunter."

"Mr. Hunter, this is Ilse with the S. Dasselaar Gallery. Mr. Dasselaar was informed you are in town and asked that I contact you to schedule a meeting. Are you available tomorrow morning at nine?"

"Yes, Ilse. Please let Mr. Dasselaar know that works perfectly for me."

"Wonderful. He looks forward to meeting you."

"And I him."

Ilse recited the address for the gallery, and I hung up.

"Well?" Hadrian asked, using the plastic key card to open the suite's door.

"We got the meeting."

CHAPTER FOUR

DIMITRI

THE CLOSER WE got to the gallery, the harder my heart beat until I was sure the huge bear shifter who worked as Dasselaar's hired muscle had to hear it. Dasselaar had left the estate early, before breakfast, but had instructed one of his goons to come get me and bring me to the gallery.

I hadn't been back since the night Dasselaar had killed the truck driver, and my stomach roiled, threatening to upend itself on the leather upholstery of his black town car as we wove closer and closer to his building in the heart of the city.

Instead of pulling up out front, the driver circled to the back of the building and parked in the alley. Dasselaar liked people to know when he was at the gallery, so he always parked out front, so I wasn't sure what was different about today, but I was praying the sense of foreboding that crawled beneath my skin was just a stress response to being back at the gallery and not a premonition that maybe I wouldn't be leaving the premises again. At least not alive.

For days, shipping crates had been arriving at the estate in preparation for the gala and auction later that week. I'd seen most of the paintings before when I'd used my talent to authenticate them for Dasselaar as they'd come into the gallery, but there was one painting I hadn't seen yet—the one the now deceased driver had delivered.

"Out." The bear shifter had come around the car and yanked open my door. "Dasselaar wants you to wait for him in the storage room."

I nodded, not trusting myself to speak around the lump in my throat and my rising panic.

Dasselaar's goon punched a code into the keypad by the door and lowered his face so the tiny embedded camera could scan his features. Since the night of the truck driver's murder, Dasselaar had also increased security at the gallery. I'd heard him talking about it when he didn't think I was listening, like when we were in the car or while I was in the dining room eating breakfast at the other end of his massive antique table.

The goon—I never knew their names—held the door for me, and secured it behind me. My heart was in my throat as my eyes fell to where the truck driver's body had been.

But there was nothing there.

The floor was painted a glossy gray just like it always had been. Not a speck of blood marred the surface.

Had I really seen someone die in this room? How could there not be a trace of the crime left behind?

A shudder rolled down my spine, and I clenched my fists at my sides to keep myself from shaking apart. I willed myself to look anywhere but at where the body had been.

Only a single shipping crate remained in the room, and I knew that was why I'd been summoned.

The bear shifter who'd brought me to the gallery today stalked by me, walking farther into the gallery. When I started to follow he held up his hand. "Dasselaar wants you to wait here."

"Oh, right. Yes. I forgot." Really, I didn't want to stay in the room swirling with the ghosts of what I'd seen by myself. But as with everything else in my life, I had no choice.

I positioned myself against the wall and leaned into it, and I waited.

And waited.

And waited.

Beyond the wall that separated the storage room from the rest of the building, I heard Dasselaar talking to one of the sophisticated women who worked for him and served as the polished public face of the S. Dasselaar Gallery, but he still kept me waiting. It wasn't like my time had value. I was his pawn, a tool he controlled. It felt like an hour had passed before Dasselaar finally deigned to enter the storage room, flanked by my driver and another bear shifter who must have been acting as Dasselaar's bodyguard for the day.

The bear shifters each picked up a screw gun and set to work opening the crate. Dasselaar pulled out a small remote and when they lifted the lid from the container, he clicked it twice. Small red lights flashed at each corner of the crate, then winked out, going dark.

"Dimitri, you know what you need to do."

I approached the crate slowly, butterflies in my stomach. Dasselaar had been talking about auctioning off the biggest score the art world had ever seen, and I knew this was it. Everything else had been normal, run-of-the-mill, stolen art. Renoir, Degas, Van Gogh, with a few lesser-known pieces sprinkled throughout for the bidder who wanted to part with ten million or less, but I knew before I even saw the piece that this was something more.

Looking into the crate, a gasp slid past my lips. *The Evolution of Man,* the most revered, controversial, and elusive piece of stolen art known to the shifter world sat nestled in packing foam. If this painting was real, it was damn near priceless. Dasselaar was going to make more money than Midas when he offered this at his auction.

Assuming it was real.

Dasselaar hovered over my shoulder as I held my hand out. With the antitransmutative drugs coursing through my system, it was difficult to pull even the small part of my animal form that I needed to authenticate the piece forward, and I closed my eyes, reaching deep within myself to accomplish even the most subtle shift. Like it always did when I used this skill, my skin tightened, and I opened my eyes. My hand hovered over the painting, but suddenly the normal tightening felt different, my skin warming like I was in the sun. The bell at the front of the gallery rang and a voice distracted Dasselaar, making him glance away from me for a split second. In that time, a strange sheen, like the swirling colors of an oil slick on water, blurred my skin before the color resolved and my skin took on the exact hue of the paint beneath it.

It was Dasselaar's turn to gasp. "It's real." He slapped me on the back, and my hand slid to a different part of the painting. That same pearlescent sheen slid over my skin before the color became clear. Again, Dasselaar missed it. He had his phone out and held to his ear, telling whoever was on the other end that he had the real thing.

But I wasn't so sure.

My skin had never turned that shiny, mother-of-pearl color before. I'd certainly never seen my skin flicker like that. It was always very straightforward. If the painting was fake, the colors my skin picked up were cloudy, unable to settle on the exact colors. If the painting was real, the color of my skin was indiscernible from the colors on the canvas. As far as I could tell, it had something to do with the chemical composition of the paint and how it reacted with my skin. My talent was remarkably reliable as very few modern forgers had the patience or the talent to reproduce the naturally pigmented oil paints used in past centuries. Even when I ran across forgeries where the artist had taken the time to produce pigments that matched almost perfectly, my skin could detect even the most subtle differences in hue.

This was something else.

I leaned forward and studied the painting more closely, moving my hand around the frame. Each time, there was a slight hesitation, a flash of iridescence, as the color changed.

Fortunately for me, Dasselaar rarely asked me to speak, so I held my tongue, biting back my suspicions about the authenticity of the painting. He had seen what he wanted to see, and that was all there was to it. It was doubtful anything I said would sway him anyway. And any opinion that this painting maybe wasn't real wouldn't be appreciated. And my skin did pick up the colors correctly after the momentary flicker, so maybe it was real. Maybe I had too much of the antitransmutative drug in my system.

"Seal it up. Call Victor and have him bring the truck, then get this to the estate." The bear shifters nodded, and the one who'd driven me to the gallery pulled out his phone. "I'll be there as soon as possible. Do not let that crate out of your sight for a single second. Make sure it gets delivered to the auction room, then stay with it."

Both bear shifters nodded their understanding.

I stepped away from the painting, rubbing my hand, and moved silently toward the door. Dasselaar caught the movement and shook his head.

"You're not going anywhere. I have an important meeting, and you're going to be needed here. Go wait in the private gallery."

There was no reason to argue, so I did as I was told, surreptitiously staring at my hands while I moved down the hallway toward the private gallery where Dasselaar kept all his stolen merchandise. The last time I'd been in that part of the gallery building had been the day I'd seen the man I'd been sketching late at night when my nightmares pulled me from sleep. My mind caught on the images I'd drawn last night of his strong, paint-stained hands and the fantasies I'd entertained of the way his skin would feel stroking over my body as I got myself off, wishing I had a name to scream into my pillow as I came.

Movement at the end of the hallway grabbed my attention, and I stopped, blinking fast, unable to believe what I was seeing. Like my mind had conjured him up, live and in full color, was the man from my drawings. He was standing in profile, so he didn't see me, but I'd know the way his hair fell over his eyes, the strong slant of his nose, and the sharp line of his jaw anywhere. A hint of dark skin peeked out above his collar, and I knew exactly what it would look like if I could peel his shirt away.

Dasselaar pushed by me, hissing at me as he went, and blocked the man from my view. "I told you to wait in the private gallery. Don't make me tell you again."

I tried to look past him, but he'd already ushered the man down another short hall where his office was located, and he was lost from my sight. Rubbing my eyes, I tried to take stock of my body. Had the dose of the drug Dasselaar's minions had administered this morning been too strong? I didn't trust myself to know if what I had seen had been real or an apparition my mind had conjured up to deal with the stress of being back at the gallery for the first time and whatever had just happened with the painting.

The skin on my hands warmed, and I glanced down to see iridescent colors shining on my palms. I wasn't consciously trying to use my talent, and with the drugs in my system, I couldn't take my chameleon form by choice or by accident.

I closed my eyes and willed my hands to look human, but when I opened them again, the colors had only faded by a fraction.

What the hell was going on?

Ducking into the private showroom full of stolen art, I hid myself in the corner and said a silent prayer that whatever was happening would go away before Dasselaar brought his guest into the gallery and made me use my skill. I needed to stay useful to him until I could figure out a plan to get my sister out of Amsterdam.

Then everything could go to shit.

Just not now.

Please not now.

CHAPTER FIVE

QUIN

"MR. HUNTER." Stefan Dasselaar held out his hand, and I shook it. "Your reputation precedes you, of course, as I've heard much about your gallery and the work you do." He paused for a moment, waiting for me to react to his statement, but I said nothing. He frowned, then replaced the expression with a welcoming smile. "Thank you for meeting with me today. This way."

Movement over his broad shoulder caught my eye, but he ushered me out of the main part of the gallery and into his office, where he gestured for me to sit in the leather visitor's chair while he settled behind his massive desk. On a lesser man, I would have assumed the mahogany monstrosity he'd put between us was a sign he was compensating for something, but Dasselaar's bulk was well-suited to the desk. Anything smaller would have made him look ridiculous.

He set his elbows on the arms of his tufted leather chair and steepled his fingers, assessing me with sharp eyes. I crossed an ankle over my knee and smoothed out a nonexistent wrinkle in my pants as I casually draped an arm along the armrest of my chair. Two could play the arrogant game. I kept my features impassive, but I studied Dasselaar right back. He looked just like the photos I'd studied on the plane ride to Amsterdam. He had dark hair streaked with gray and white that was expensively cut and styled. He wore a designer suit, but unlike Zwart's, Dasselaar's had been perfectly tailored to fit his broad shoulders and expanding waist. The lines of a man who used to be incredibly fit still lingered along the badger shifter's frame, but they'd been liberally filled in by what could only be an excess of fine food and drink.

Another moment of charged silence passed between us, but I didn't so much as shift in my seat. Stillness was one of my superpowers. I could wait him out forever if he made me.

Luckily, that wasn't the case. He dropped his hands onto his desk. "I understand you have made Niels Zwart a great deal of money."

I shrugged nonchalantly. "It was a simple negotiation, and in fairness, Zwart didn't know what he had."

Dasselaar laughed, the sound deep and rumbling, and I almost felt it through the floor. "That is his problem more often than not, but given what he told me, it doesn't appear you took advantage of his lack of knowledge."

"There was no need. The Lichtenstein is worth every penny his buyer is going to pay for it."

Dasselaar nodded. "I regret that I didn't have the opportunity to acquire that piece for myself."

I raised an eyebrow. "That surprises me. From what I know of your gallery, you tend to favor the impressionists and neoclassical pieces."

"You've done your research." He smoothed his hands over his blotter. "You are not wrong. Nineteenth-century art is a weakness of mine. But to acquire a rare Lichtenstein would have been a thrill."

"The market for pop art outside of Warhol is tricky."

He laughed again, quieter this time. "Indeed it is." He sat back in his chair and steepled his fingers again. "But my instincts tell me you are not in Amsterdam to discuss the art markets."

"You're right. I'm not. I was in town on business, meeting with several European contacts, as you know, since one of those contacts reached out to you."

"And what exactly are you hoping to get from your time in Amsterdam?"

"Besides the one point two million dollars from closing Zwart's deal, you mean?"

Dasselaar's lips twitched and he nodded.

"I'm looking to increase my European client base, and Zwart mentioned you were hosting an event that might facilitate that goal."

"Zwart mentioned it?"

"He did."

The badger shifter's eyes narrowed as he tried to suss out whether I was telling the truth about Zwart dropping a mention of Dasselaar's gala into our conversation or if I knew because he'd invited Juno. "Interesting."

My heartbeat picked up a little. Was there a chance Dasselaar knew why we were really here? "How so?"

"I invited your grandmother to the event Zwart mentioned."

I schooled my features into a mask of slight surprise. "Did you?"

He inclined his head, scrutinizing me in a way that made me want to squirm, but I held still, doing my best to remain coolly professional. This was my first interaction with Dasselaar, but I was getting the sense he was already suspicious of my intent. Even though Cal and I looked pretty different from one another, it was impossible to deny the similarities, and Dasselaar wasn't stupid. If he recognized me and made the connection to Cal, this op was dead in the water. He already knew I was connected to Juno and had since before I'd set foot on Dutch soil.

Dasselaar sat forward in his chair abruptly, reaching for the phone on his desk. The hairs on the back of my neck stood on end and he lifted the receiver to his ear and hit a button on the lit panel. Was he calling his security team to have me removed from the premises? Had I managed to blow the op? What misstep had I made?

But he wasn't calling his security team. "Ilse, please bring the guest list for the gala and your notes to my office."

He reset the handset in the cradle and returned to studying me.

Ilse walked through his office door a few moments later and set a blue file folder on his desk. He flipped it open, and I clenched my muscles to keep from leaning over the papers to see his guest list. Felix and Julius had still been unsuccessful in securing a copy.

Dasselaar ran his finger down the list. "Here. I sent her

two invitations. One to her address in Alaska and a second via your gallery."

Shit, shit, shit.

"Juno has been out of town for the better part of the month. Any mail she's received has been left for her to address when she returns. If I did receive something on her behalf, I wouldn't have paid it much attention."

"So she will not be attending?"

"Not unless you also sent an invitation via carrier pigeon to the cruise ship she's on in the middle of the Pacific."

To my great relief, Dasselaar laughed. "I assume she's enjoying her retirement?"

"Seems like it."

Dasselaar went quiet, and I felt his gaze attempting to bore into me, so I pulled my professional armor a little tighter and gave him no quarter. After another long moment, he relaxed. "I'd like to show you something." He pushed his bulk out of his chair and stood, waiting for me to do the same.

My heart hammered against my ribs so loudly I wondered if Dasselaar could hear it. I mentally crossed my fingers that what he wanted to show me wasn't a pair of custom-made cement shoes at the edge of one of Amsterdam's famous canals. For a second, I wished I'd taken Nero and Cal up on their offer to give me a comm device so they'd know what was happening.

Instead of taking me outside, he led me back into the main part of the gallery where Ilse was talking to a couple in front of a lovely landscape of the Dutch countryside covered in a carpet of bright red tulips. She smiled my way before I turned, following Dasselaar down a hallway that appeared to lead to the rear of the building.

He led me down a hallway toward the back of the building, then into a private gallery. The second I crossed the threshold, I knew why he was showing me this space. Every one of the dozen paintings that hung on the walls was stolen. I recognized each on sight, including a Renoir that had a small red sold sign hanging next to it. Cal had told me he and Jack had agreed to purchase *Madeleine Leaning on her Elbow with Flowers in her Hair*. It wasn't my favorite Renoir, but it was the first time I'd seen it in person. The general public tended to assume paintings by the masters were mostly displayed in museums around the world. In reality, a lot of fine art was maintained in private collections. The Renoir I was looking at had been stolen from one such collection during a completely unsophisticated smash-and-grab job over a decade ago and had never been recovered. I dealt with stolen art every day, but coming across pieces I knew were stolen never ceased to surprise me. In this case, I knew Dasselaar had the Renoir, but to see it hanging in his gallery half a world away from where it had been taken was surreal, to say the least. It should have come through me before it ever got to him. And if it had, it wouldn't be the original that was hanging on the wall. It would be my forgery.

"Unfortunately, that particular piece has already been sold." Dasselaar had noticed where my eye had immediately gone.

"I've never had the privilege of seeing this painting in

person. Forgive me in advance for the question I'm about to ask, but is it authentic?"

A sly smile spread across Dasselaar's lips. "It is." He gestured to the room at large. "They all are."

I ran a quick mental tally. Assuming each of the twelve pieces in the room went for current market value, I was surrounded by over three hundred million dollars in stolen art. There were blank spaces on the wall where other pieces must have hung, and I wondered if the missing items would be making an appearance at the gala.

Moving slowly around the room, I studied each piece. Dasselaar's inventory was a checklist of some of Interpol's top unsolved thefts, and the part of me that had been raised by a master art and antiquities thief was dying to know how Dasselaar had come to be in possession of so many pieces.

But I didn't let the question fall past my lips.

"They are all authentic, you say?"

"Do you doubt it?"

I tilted my head in a gesture meant to convey that I wasn't convinced either way.

"Dimitri, come here."

A young man who appeared to be in his early to mid-twenties stepped out from behind a partition wall at the back of the gallery. Brilliant chartreuse eyes flashed as they met mine, colors swirling through them so fast it made me dizzy even from across the room. He was tall, only a few inches shorter than me, though he stood with his shoulders slightly rounded as though he was trying to make himself smaller. He was slim and wiry, but as he moved toward us, I was taken in by the subtle grace of his movements. His body moved like silk flowing in a gentle breeze, and I thought I could watch him walk forever. He could make a killing working a runway in Paris or Milan, and that was before considering the absolute perfection of his face. His smooth, unblemished skin was a stunning bronze that almost seemed to glow in the overhead light. He had black hair that shone with shades of blue and green as he came closer, and I had to wonder if the colors I was seeing were natural or another trick of the light. The line of his jaw was sharp enough to cut glass and clean-shaven, and the planes of his aquiline nose spoke of Mediterranean heritage. His plush lips were full, the top one just a little thinner than the bottom, and a deep dusky pink, that made me think he spent a lot of time biting them.

I wanted to bite them.

But it was his eyes that held me captive more than anything. His bright green eyes were round and outlined with thick, dark lashes. They'd widened slightly when he'd noticed I was standing with Dasselaar, taking me in like he recognized me but was surprised to see me there. As he closed the last of the distance between us, his eyes never left mine, and it felt like his gaze reached through me and touched my soul.

The bottom dropped out of my stomach as he continued to stare at me, and for all I knew or cared Dasselaar had faded away into nothingness. Dimitri was all that mattered. He was so beautiful, and I ached to feel his skin under my fingers—to feel his body wrapped around mine—with an intensity I hadn't felt for anything but my art in a long, long time. I'd never been hit by a craving as deep as the one that coiled in my belly, begging me to pull the younger man closer.

To keep him safe.

To claim him as my own.

That final thought made my breath catch in my chest as Dasselaar snapped at the man.

"Dimitri. Now." Dasselaar's tone made a growl rise up in my chest and my hands ball into fists. I bit back the primitive sound and relaxed my hands, unwilling to give away my reaction as I felt Dasselaar's eyes on me as Dimitri moved across the room.

When Dimitri stopped in front of us where we stood next to a Cezanne landscape, Dasselaar gestured to the painting. Dimitri stepped forward and held out his hand, long fingers shaking as he lifted them toward the painting.

"The boy has a gift." Dasselaar sounded like the predator he truly was behind the fine art and his farce of a gallery. "If a painting is authentic, Dimitri's skin can adapt to the colors on the canvas."

As I watched, the young man's skin turned from a natural bronze to match the varied shades of green in the landscape. His hand almost disappeared, blending seamlessly into the colors of the painting.

When it came to art, I'd seen almost everything, but what Dimitri was doing was extraordinary. It left me nearly breathless. Dimitri wiggled his fingers and moved his hand around the canvas. The second he was still for more than a moment, the colors on his skin shifted adapting to whatever hues were under his palm.

Cal had tried to explain Dimitri's talent to me, but he hadn't done it justice at all.

"Fascinating." I heard myself breathe the word without meaning to, and the young man's gaze swung my way. When his eyes connected with mine, it felt like he was looking directly into my soul, and I never wanted him to look away.

Dasselaar grabbed his arm and pulled him away from the painting, and while I was typically not a violent person, I had the sudden urge to break every bone in every one of Dasselaar's fingers where they gripped Dimitri's bicep. Again, my fists clenched at my sides, and I breathed through the intense anger that flooded my veins seeing someone else's hands on something that was mine.

Mine?

Dimitri wasn't mine.

There was no way.

But my hand rubbed over my neck where the dark skin of my saddle patch was mostly concealed by my shirt. I was desperate to rip the fabric away so I could see if my reaction to Dimitri meant what I thought it might.

That he was my fated mate.

"Get the Vermeer." Dasselaar let go of Dimitri and shoved him away. He went to the corner of the room where a partition was cleverly concealed and stepped behind it. When he was gone from view, my heart twisted in my chest. He returned a second later, a framed painting in hand.

Dasselaar took it from his hands and turned it to face me. An incredible forgery of Vermeer's *Girl with a Pearl Earring* stared back at me. To the untrained eye, it would have looked one hundred percent authentic, but I had spent years studying the way each of the masters put paint on their canvases, and the angle of the brush strokes was off by the tiniest fraction. While I knew the painting Dasselaar held was fake, I had no doubt the majority of art authenticators would have certified the painting as a genuine Vermeer.

"Show him." Dasselaar nodded to the painting.

Dimitri had been watching me examine the painting, but at Dasselaar's command, he stepped forward again, his hand outstretched. This time when his palm hovered over the painting, the colors on his skin split into shades that weren't on the canvas like his skin couldn't quite match the color. The rapid shift in hue made the colors that flashed on Dimitri's skin seem cloudy.

"Since I'm sure you have a keen eye, you've no doubt recognized the Vermeer as an excellent forgery, but a forgery nonetheless. When a modern artist attempts to reproduce a piece, the medium is often a mix of several types of contemporary paint meant to mimic the shade, texture, and age of the original. Dimitri's skin can detect those anomalies, leading to this." He nodded to where Dimitri's hand was still clearly visible in front of the painting. Unlike when he'd done the same with the Cezanne, this time the differences between the tones on his skin and the paint on the canvas were obvious.

Dasselaar passed the painting to Dimitri, who took it, stumbling a little under the weight of the frame, and disappeared to put it back behind the partition.

"That was fascinating and immensely helpful when it comes to your business pursuits, no doubt." I spoke to Dasselaar but kept my eyes on where Dimitri had disappeared, hoping he would reemerge so I could see him again.

"Indeed." Dasselaar brushed off his hands. "Now that you understand the caliber of merchandise in my collection, let's talk about what you can do to help me get these pieces and those purchased at my gala shipped without detection."

CHAPTER SIX

QUIN

"WE GOT THE INVITE. Let's get back to the hotel so we can debrief."

I was also going to need to pack. Dasselaar had invited me to join him at his estate for the weekend, which just solidified my gut feeling that he was suspicious and trying to keep an eye on me.

Hadrian pushed off the sleek black car where he'd been leaning, basking in the afternoon sunlight while he waited for me to finish my meeting with Dasselaar. He opened the rear passenger-side door for me, and I slid into the car.

Climbing behind the wheel, my cousin smiled at me through the rearview mirror. "Nice work."

He put the car in drive and left me to my thoughts as he wound through the narrow streets. My mind should have been on my meeting with Dasselaar or working out what I needed to do to prepare for three nights at his estate. Instead, my thoughts were full of wide green eyes, tousled black hair, plush lips, and skin that looked as smooth as

Italian marble, skin I wanted to run my fingers over. Lips I had the unreasonable urge to kiss.

I'd never in my whole life been sucker punched by lust like I had been the minute I'd seen Dimitri. And it wasn't just the raging desire to hold him in my arms or to feel his naked skin against mine that had me unsettled. I wanted to open the buttons on my shirt to see if my saddle patch had changed, if Dimitri was fated to be mine, but I wasn't sure I could handle the disappointment if my reaction to him was nothing but lust fueled by the adrenaline of this mission. And what would I do if my saddle patch had changed, if Dimitri was meant for me? I wasn't sure I could stop myself from begging Hadrian to turn the car around so I could run into the gallery and steal Dimitri away.

A latent protective and possessive streak had ignited in my core, and above all else, I wanted to keep him safe.

I hated the way Dasselaar treated Dimitri, and I wondered why Dimitri continued to work for him when it was clear Dasselaar was just using him. My blood started to boil when I replayed the rough way Dasselaar had handled the younger man. I could have killed the badger shifter for daring to put his hands on what was mine. Remembering the scene had my hands clenching into angry fists. Drawing in a deep breath, I willed myself to relax. Hadrian glanced at me in the mirror again and gave me a reassuring smile, but he said nothing. Before he'd met his mate—a beaver shifter art professor who was only a little obsessed with our grandmother—my cousin had spent a lot of time alone doing legitimate salvage diving work for the police and not-so-legal salvage diving and treasure hunting for fun. He was a man of few words, which suited my mood right now just fine.

The reality was Dimitri wasn't mine, and I needed to get over whatever the hell had happened in the gallery. I needed to get my head in the game.

But thoughts of Dimitri wouldn't be willed away.

Desperate to find out what Cal and Jack knew about him, I was out of the car and hitting the button to call the elevator almost before Hadrian put the car in park. My cousin caught up with me as the shiny bronze doors slid open, and he followed me inside.

"What happened in there?" Hadrian's question pulled me out of my thoughts and I turned to look at him.

I rubbed a hand over my face. "I don't really know. Dasselaar has a young man working for him, and he just took me by surprise."

Hadrian raised an eyebrow. "Surprised you how?" My fingers toyed with the collar of my shirt, and his eyes tracked the movement, going wide when he pieced together what I wasn't saying.

"I don't know."

"Let me see." Hadrian reached for the collar of my shirt so he could slide it aside and look at my saddle patch to see if it had changed, but the elevator stopped and the doors slid open before he made contact.

Cal was pacing in the hallway, and when the doors slid open, his head swung to look at us. "What the fuck happened? I felt something strange through our twin bond. I thought you were hurt." He looked me over from head to toe, then put his hands on my shoulders and turned me around, looking at me from every angle. "Are you hurt?"

Shrugging out of his touch, I took a step away. "I'm fine. I got the invitation."

"You did?" His eyes were still scanning me like he didn't believe I was telling him the truth.

"Why the tone of surprise?"

Cal held his hands up in mock surrender. "No, I'm not surprised. I knew you could do it." He used his keycard to open the suite door, and Hadrian and I followed him inside. The suite was a hub of activity. Since we'd arrived, the suite had been transformed from a luxury penthouse to a command center. Felix and Julius had commandeered the dining table and had set up their laptops. Jack and Nero were sitting on the couch in the living room area looking over a set of blueprints for Dasselaar's estate, which they'd somehow managed to acquire, that was spread out on the coffee table. Everyone looked up when we entered the room.

"Are we good to go?" Julius asked, and it felt like everyone was holding their breath as they waited for my answer.

"We are."

"Excellent." Nero rubbed his hands together.

"But there is a small change of plans." Movement around the room stopped, and every eye was on me. "According to the invitation, the gala is Saturday night, but Dasselaar invited me to join him at his estate, with a select group of VIPs, beginning tomorrow night. I'm supposed to arrive in time for dinner and stay through brunch following the gala."

Jack tapped the blueprints on the table. "Oh, this is good. Very, very good. It's impossible to know if these plans are accurate since they only show the original building and don't detail any upgrades or changes that might have been made since Dasselaar acquired the property. A man on the inside is exactly what we need."

Nero considered what he said and raised his eyebrows. "Jack makes an excellent point. We thought having you as a guest at the gala would give us a visual during the party and auction, but having you there to do recon before the event is honestly even better."

"This changes the plan." Jack sat back on the couch, his mind already working through the new details.

My older brother's focus returned to me. "Did you see the painting today? Cal and Jack said it was at the gallery."

"No. Dasselaar has over a quarter of a billion dollars of stolen art in his private gallery, but none of the pieces on display were *The Evolution of Man*." I scoffed. "Don't you think if I'd seen the painting I would have led with that?"

"Okay, fair." Nero shifted on the couch. "Did you see anything else?"

For a second, I wanted to tell him about how I'd felt meeting Dimitri, but something made me hold back. Cal's eyes met mine as I looked away from Nero, and it was almost like he could read my thoughts, even though I'd always been better at reading his through our twin bond. Ignoring the strange sensation, I looked at Nero again. "Not anything that will help. I only caught a brief glimpse of the storage room, and it looked empty from what I could see."

Jack spoke up again. "That tracks with what we've seen. He's been moving pieces to his estate. *The Evolution of Man* was the only piece we hadn't accounted for yet, but it makes sense that he'd move it by itself."

"I wish I had seen more, but besides Dasselaar's office and the gallery filled with stolen art, I wasn't given a behind-the-scenes tour."

"That's fine. The estate is the target anyway, and now that you'll be there for a couple days before the gala, you'll be able to close the circle on a lot of the things we need to know." Nero turned back to the blueprints on the table. "We're going to need you to walk around the house and the grounds as much as you can without making Dasselaar suspicious."

It was on the tip of my tongue to tell him that I thought Dasselaar was already suspicious, but like telling him about Dimitri, I bit the words back. I didn't want them to call off the op. Not yet. And I thought if they knew I suspected Dasselaar was onto the fact that we were up to something, Nero would pull the plug.

"While you guys strategize, Quinny and I need to talk." Cal had taken a seat on the other sofa in the living room and had been studying me as Nero conducted his inquisition. He pushed to his feet and grabbed my arm, towing me into the room he was sharing with Jack. He closed the door behind us and flipped the lock. When I gave him a questioning look, he shrugged. "I don't think you want an audience for this."

"For what?" I crossed my arms, and my twin mirrored the movement.

"Take off your shirt."

"What? Why?"

"Because I need to see something." Cal reached for me, but I dodged him.

"I'm not taking off my shirt."

"Quintillus, if I have to hold you down and rip it off you, I will."

"You wouldn't dare, *Caligula*. This is Paul Smith."

Cal's jaw went tight at my use of his full first name, but he gave me no quarter. "I don't know who that is, and I don't care. Strip."

"No. Stop being weird."

"I'm not being weird. I just want to see."

"See what?"

"Your saddle patch." He blew out an exasperated breath. "If you won't take off your shirt, at least let me see it."

"Why?" But I already knew. I'd known since the second Dimitri's big green eyes had met mine.

"It's a hunch."

I wanted to know too, but I was afraid to look. I'd been hoping to find my fated mate for a long, long time, and if this wasn't it—if Dimitri wasn't it—I couldn't explain why I wanted him so badly after a single meeting where we hadn't spoken a single word to one another and I'd had to pretend I was indifferent to his presence in front of Dasselaar.

"Fine." My fingers shook as I undid the first few buttons on my shirt. Cal's patience snapped, and he pushed the fabric away before I could.

He gasped. "I fucking knew it."

Shoving him out of the way, I made a beeline for the bathroom, ignoring the wet towel and dirty clothes on the floor. Closing my eyes for a second, I took a deep breath, then opened them and pushed my shirt aside so I could see my saddle patch. The solid stretch of black skin had changed, the darker patch now split into a wide, deep vee that looked like a thick brushstroke. My fingers traced over the skin, and I saw Cal leaning in the bathroom doorway, arms crossed over his chest and a smug look on his face.

"You met Dimitri today, didn't you?" My twin's expression was fond when he said Dimitri's name.

Shocked, I nodded. "How did you know?"

Cal shook his head. "I knew something big happened to you today, but I couldn't tell what. At first, I thought you were hurt or that Dasselaar figured out what we're planning—"

Holding up a hand, I cut him off. "I think he's suspicious. He doesn't need me to move merchandise for him. Even if he wants to send a few of his clients through me to avoid moving it all himself, he didn't have to invite me for the weekend. I think he's trying to keep me close so he can figure out if I'm up to something."

My twin chewed on his lip for a second. "Does it matter? We now have you on the inside for days before the gala. Even if he's trying to keep you close just to keep an eye on you, it helps us out."

"If you say so."

"I do. And I'm not as stupid as you seem to think I am. I see what you did there with the subject change."

I turned back to my reflection in the mirror. "How did you know it was Dimitri?"

"When I met him, I felt oddly drawn to him, like I wanted to keep him safe but not for myself. It's like how I feel about Jack but much less intense. I didn't know what it meant then, but when I felt the surge of emotion in our bond, I knew."

"What do we know about him?" My eyes still lingered on my saddle patch as I braced my palms on the counter and leaned forward.

"Unfortunately, not much. Felix has been trying to find him, but we don't have a last name, and he doesn't come up on our list of Dasselaar's known associates."

"What am I supposed to do?"

"About?" Cal looked genuinely concerned.

"About Dimitri. My gut tells me he's a pawn in all this, but what if I'm wrong?"

Cal gave me a sad smile. "I don't think you're wrong. I think Dasselaar has some kind of hold on him, but without a last name, we can't figure out what."

"I assume he's going to be at the gala. Did you know he can change his skin to match an authentic painting? It's fascinating. His skin just changes to the exact hues on the canvas, but it doesn't work if the piece is a forgery. I've never seen anything like it."

"I know. I've seen it too, and I think it is safe to assume Dasselaar is going to want to show off his special skills at the gala as a sort of live authentication."

"That makes sense." I turned away from the mirror and leaned my hip against the vanity.

"Hopefully he's one of Dasselaar's guests at the estate."

"And what? I'm supposed to walk up to him and tell him he's my fated mate?"

Cal laughed. "No. I mean, not if you don't want to. It took me the better part of two years to tell Jack. But you could get to know him a little bit. Find out who he is." An odd emotion flickered through our twin bond, and I knew Cal wasn't telling me something.

"What don't I know?" My twin said nothing, but that weird feeling still vibrated down our bond and I didn't like it.

"Nothing." Cal pretended to look at a watch he didn't wear and pushed off the doorframe. "You should start packing."

Over the next day, Nero, Cal, Jack, and Hadrian came up with a list of information they needed that they thought I could obtain while inside Dasselaar's estate. They'd made me memorize the list and recite it over and over again. I could tell Nero was nervous about not being able to plan the heist before sending me in, but there were too many loose ends and too many variables, and until I provided them with onsite intel, their planning was dead in the water. As it stood, we weren't even sure where Dasselaar was housing the painting. Nero would have to come up with a final plan on the fly after I gave him more to work with.

The door to the suite opened and Cal and Jack sauntered in. They were both wearing dark blue coveralls that had the logo for a Dutch electricity provider embroidered on the chest.

Nero, who'd been pacing by the window, turned to look at them. "So?"

"Felix was right. The power for Dasselaar's security system routes all the way to the street. We were able to install the piggyback so we can control his power and get into the cameras."

"Excellent." Felix rubbed his hands together like a cartoon villain, then linked his fingers together and turned his palms out, cracking his knuckles before his hands started flying over his keyboard.

A few minutes later, Felix shouted in triumph, startling Cal who had been stepping out of his coveralls. He started to fall, but Jack steadied him before he hit the floor. "Careful, sweetheart." Cal beamed up at Jack, who placed a small kiss on his temple.

Nero crossed the room to stand behind his mate, his large hands massaging Felix's shoulders. "What do you have?"

"I'm a little shocked it was this easy to get into his system. He's got cameras throughout his estate, and they're decent quality, but on the whole, the system is pretty basic."

"That's good for us, though, right?" Hadrian asked. He had hung back from most of the conversations, content to text with his mate, Ben, until he was needed for a specific task.

"Yes and no." Nero leaned forward to take a closer look at Felix's computer. "I've seen this before. People who have a basic security system usually have other methods of keeping themselves and their belongings safe."

Jack nodded. "He's relying on personnel."

Nero tapped his nose and pointed at Jack. "Yep, and it's a lot harder to get around people than to hack into a sophisticated security system. No offense, Lucky." He dropped a kiss on his mate's head.

Felix turned to look up at him, and Nero's lips dropped

to Felix's in a quick kiss. "None taken. And for what it's worth, I think you're right. Four different scary-looking dudes have walked through this hall alone since I got into the feed."

We all circled the table, standing behind Felix and watching the camera angles.

"That's a lot of manpower." Julius held up a Post-it note where he'd drawn tally marks. "I count at least fifteen different guys."

"We need to know if they're on specific patrols or if they are just randomly walking the estate." Cal looked a little concerned, and I felt it in our twin bond. Did he think I wouldn't be able to handle this?

"I have something that will help us get a better lay of the land." Felix shooed us away so he could slide his chair back and stand up, and we all dispersed back to where we'd been before Felix had hacked the video feed. He disappeared into the bedroom he and Nero were sharing, and a minute later, he returned to the living room carrying two small leather ring boxes. Felix set them down on the table, then picked up the top one and flipped it open, showing me what was inside. "I've been tinkering with these to help me sleep and because I knew we were going to need a video feed at some point. I put the finishing touches on it last night and now we just need to test it."

A small, onyx pin sat nestled in black velvet. It was a Haida-style orca that was quite lovely, but I didn't understand what I was supposed to do with it.

"It's a camera. I made it black so it would blend in with your preferred wardrobe. When you put it on, we'll be able to see whatever you're seeing." He set the case down and carefully pulled the pin out, then spoke over his shoulder to Julius who was still behind his computer at the dining room table. "Jules, can you bring over my computer so I can calibrate the image and test the feed?"

"Aye, aye, Quartermaster." Julius gave him a mock salute, then picked up Felix's laptop and brought it over. Felix handed me the pin. "Put it on your lapel. That should give us the best angle."

I looked at the pin, then at Felix. "You want me to put a pinhole in this suit?"

Felix stared at me like I was stupid. "Yes. Is that a problem?"

"This is Tom Ford."

Felix crossed his arms. "And I'm Felix White. I don't have time to rework the camera into anything else."

Glancing down my body, I noted the striped pocket square I'd placed earlier. It too was designer but far easier to replace than the suit. "How about here?" I tapped the pocket square. Can I put it here?"

Felix shrugged and shoved his glasses up his nose.

I was still going to have to pierce my suit, but hopefully the pinhole wouldn't be as noticeable if it wasn't on the lapel. Reluctantly, I pushed the pin into the fabric, securing it on the fold of the pocket while Felix and Julius did whatever they needed to do on Felix's computer to ensure the image was coming through clearly.

When they were satisfied, Felix handed me the case. "The charger is inside. As long as you put the pin in the case overnight, you'll have enough power to transmit video all day." Felix reached for my jacket and removed the pin, placing it back in the case.

"Okay." I nodded to the other case. "What's in there?"

"Standard issue closed-channel comms. With a slight twist." He flipped the case open to reveal a heavy silver ring with a light amber-colored stone. "The stone pops out, and it goes in your ear." He demonstrated and handed me the earpiece. "Make sure it fits."

I slipped the device into my ear. "It feels good." My voice echoed back to me with a slight delay from Felix's laptop.

"And it seems like the sound is relaying well too." Felix fiddled with his laptop for a second, then disappeared into the room he was sharing with Nero and closed the door. A second later, I heard his voice in my ear. "Quin, can you hear me?"

"Loud and clear."

"Excellent."

Felix returned to the living room and held out his hand. I took the comm device from my ear and placed it in his palm. He popped it back into the ring and put the ring back into the leather box. "This has a fantastic transmission range, so we should be able to hear you whenever you're wearing the comm." He held up the leather box. "The charger is in here. If Dasselaar does some kind of security screening, these devices should just look like jewelry in your bags."

"Is it my turn to give Quin something?" Cal emerged from his bedroom with three hard-sided cases. "Take your pick, Quinny."

I shook my head. "I don't need a gun."

"Oh yes, you do. We don't know who else is going to be there, and you might need it. I'd prefer you had some way to defend yourself beyond your rapier wit." Cal smirked at his joke, then gestured at the cases again. "Pick or I'll pick for you."

He wasn't going to let this go, so I blindly picked a case and prayed I wouldn't have to use what was inside.

CHAPTER SEVEN

DIMITRI

"WELCOME, WELCOME." Dasselaar's voice boomed from the driveway, audible even through my closed window.

I'd been daydreaming about the man from the gallery.

Again.

In fact, there had been little on my mind since.

At first, I hadn't been able to believe what I was seeing. It couldn't be true that the man I'd been dreaming about was a real person, but there he'd been, and when he looked at me, it was as though he was looking into my soul. There was no other way to explain the way it had felt when our eyes connected across Dasselaar's private gallery.

Moving to the window, I looked down into the courtyard where a limo and two black town cars were parked in front of the house. While I watched, Dasselaar offered a hand to the person in the limo and an elegant hand adorned with a large emerald ring took it before a gorgeous Asian woman stepped from the car. Her black hair was cut into a chic bob and the emerald green dress she wore perfectly matched her ring and fit her as though it had been made for her. Her eyes were covered with large dark sunglasses and she confidently pulled her hand from Dasselaar's as soon as she was out of the vehicle. He led her to the door and introduced her to a member of his staff who ushered her into the house while her valet retrieved her bags from the trunk.

Dasselaar returned to the line of cars as a member of Dasselaar's security team directed the limo out of the drive. A tall man in military dress emerged from the second vehicle. I was too far away to make out any of the insignia on his chest. He laughed at something Dasselaar said and responded in heavily accented English.

The third car held an older man dressed in a simple gray suit. He was sour-faced and seemed to barely acknowledge Dasselaar as he greeted him. Two large bodyguards flanked the man as Dasselaar led them to the door. There was a brief conversation, and the bodyguards were turned away, the sour-faced man and his bodyguards looking none too pleased about being separated.

For the next hour, I stared out the window watching as a veritable who's who of the wealthy elite and criminal underworld arrived at the estate. But there was only one person I was waiting to see.

Noise in the halls told me members of Dasselaar's staff were getting his guests situated in the suites on the floors below mine. No one would be staying on this floor. Dasselaar made sure I was isolated so no one suspected I was being held against my will.

The sun was starting to set when yet another nondescript but expensive black town car pulled into the drive. My heart turned over in my chest, and I knew even before the car came to a stop in front of the house that the man from the gallery was inside. I wished more than anything that I knew his name.

Dasselaar appeared from the front door as the car came to a stop and the driver hopped out, opening the rear door so the man from the gallery could get out. He was as beautiful as he was in my dreams and in my memories from the gallery. He wore a navy blue suit that fit him perfectly, molding to the planes and angles of his body. His dark hair shone in the setting sun, painting the black strands with shades of gold and vermillion, and I prayed to a deity that had never listened to me before and likely wouldn't start now that he was here for me. He and Dasselaar spoke as the man's driver unloaded his suitcase from the car, and I silently begged him to look up at me, to see me in the window.

As if my wish had been granted, he glanced up so I could see his full face, and his lips tipped into a slow smile when his gaze found my window. My stomach swooped and my heart ached with longing. I wanted to stare at him all night, but scraping in the lock on my door made me look away.

"Mr. Dasselaar would like you to dress for dinner with his guests." I'd long since stopped asking the names of the goons Dasselaar sent to drug me and relay his commands, but this particular goon, another bear shifter, had a jagged scar that ran from his temple to the corner of his mouth, so I'd taken to calling him Scar in my mind. He was one of the worst guards Dasselaar had put on my detail. He was never remotely kind, and in my opinion, he took sick pleasure in stabbing me with the needle when it was his turn to administer my daily dose of antitransmutative drugs. I also hated the way his eyes lingered over me. His leering made my skin crawl, and I was grateful Dasselaar always sent his men in teams of two. Even with Scar's bulky frame blocking the door, I could sense the other guard in the hallway.

"You're supposed to wear the dark gray suit. You have thirty minutes to get ready. If you aren't ready when we return, we've been instructed to leave you in your room where you will not receive an evening meal." Scar said the last part with undisguised glee as though the thought of me going hungry made him happy. He said nothing else but hesitated in the doorway, staring at me like he was waiting for me to start stripping right there in front of him.

"You can go. I need to get ready."

Scar waited for another second, but when I didn't move, keeping my arms crossed firmly over my chest, he stepped back and closed the door. The key scraped in the lock again. I immediately returned to the window, but the man from the gallery and the car that had brought him to the estate were both gone.

My hands warmed, and I looked down to see the iridescent glow I'd first noticed when I'd examined *The Evolution of Man* at the gallery flash across my skin. The glow had been occurring consistently since then, but I was no closer to figuring out what it was than I had been the first time I saw it. Then again, it wasn't like I had any way to research the phenomenon. Dasselaar never let me into his library or near a computer, and I was only allowed to speak to my sister on the phone once a week. Those calls were always conducted under Dasselaar's supervision, and he'd end them abruptly if he thought I was saying too much—or if I lapsed into our native Greek—so I hadn't been able to ask her.

I'd gotten lost in my head, and my time was slipping by. I needed to see the man from the gallery up close, so there was no way I was going to miss dinner. I was just pulling on the suit jacket when the door handle rattled and Scar's face appeared in the doorway.

"You're ready." There was a hint of disappointment in his voice like it would have made him happy to close the door and leave me to starve for the evening.

"I am."

He pushed the door open wider and let me slip into the hall. As always, a familiar rush of freedom coursed through me when I stepped over the threshold. I was still being closely guarded, one of Dasselaar's musclebound goons flanking me on either side, but I was outside my room, and that was something. A gilded prison was still a prison.

Delicious scents wafted up the stairs, and my mouth watered. Dasselaar's cook was excellent, and I knew she would have pulled out all the stops in preparing this weekend's menu. I started to rush forward into the dining room, but Scar grabbed my wrist, squeezing tightly.

"What?" I tried to twist my arm free, but he held me tighter.

"Dasselaar wants you to wait until all the guests are seated. Your place is at the far end of the table near the kitchen. You're to enter through there."

I hadn't seen much of Dasselaar's estate, but I'd seen enough to know Dasselaar had modernized the house from its eighteenth-century origins and had brought the kitchen out of the cellar and onto the first floor, connecting it to the grand dining room through a large butler's pantry. I knew why he wanted me to slip in through the kitchen entrance. I was nothing more than the help. What I failed to understand was why he wanted me to attend this dinner at all. He could have had a tray sent up to my room. I didn't need to be there.

But I wanted to be there because the man from the gallery would be there. Maybe if I listened hard enough I would be able to catch his name.

My palms tingled, and I knew if I looked at them I'd see the strange glow around my fingers, so I shoved my hands into my pockets and let Scar and the other guard lead me into the kitchen.

Scar watched through the door, then pushed it open just enough for me to slip through so I could take my spot at the head of the table opposite Dasselaar, who was seated at the other end. This was always our arrangement whenever I had the misfortune of sharing a meal with him. Dasselaar kept an eagle eye on me as if he expected me to steal a steak knife and attempt to stab him with it. And while I might have considered it more than once, I wouldn't risk Athina's life that way, so I dutifully lowered into the chair that had become my dedicated seat as the rest of the guests took their places. I assumed no one had seen me enter the room, but when I looked up I found familiar dark eyes watching me.

The man from the gallery was seated across from me at the far end of the table where Dasselaar could observe us both from his position. The seat at the end of the table on our side conspicuously left vacant with no place setting indicating there was going to be another guest.

My heartbeat picked up speed as I looked at the face I knew so well. He smiled at me, and my stomach fluttered. He started to open his mouth, hopefully to tell me his name, but Dasselaar stood and launched into a speech welcoming everyone to his estate and promising an exciting weekend ahead. Then he clapped his hands, like the total arrogant asshole he was, and four tuxedoed servers came in through the door off the foyer. It was completely impractical to serve dinner that way, but Dasselaar was attempting to make an impression.

A bowl of orange soup with a swirl of green was set in front of me.

"Ginger carrot soup with basil oil." The server leaned in closer to my ear and whispered. "Mr. Dasselaar asked me to remind you that you are furniture, and furniture does not speak, even when spoken to."

"I understand." The words were mumbled under my breath, for the server's ears only, but I felt the man across the table's eyes on me as the server stood and walked away. That also explained why Dasselaar had left the set between us unoccupied. For as arrogant as Dasselaar was, he wasn't stupid. He clearly didn't want me close enough to the man who had haunted my dreams and fantasies to be able to speak to him.

Any excitement I'd felt at getting to see the man from the gallery, at the thought that I might get to talk to him, evaporated along with my appetite. I lifted my eyes only long enough to see Dasselaar watching me. He picked up his spoon and wiggled it in the air, indicating I should do the same. I didn't want to. Refusing to pick up the spoon would be a tiny act of rebellion, but I felt Scar standing behind me, and I didn't want to risk the consequences. I didn't think Dasselaar would have Scar rough me up, not when he needed me pretty and presentable for what he had planned for tomorrow, but Scar could always hurt me where the bruises wouldn't show. He'd done it before.

Grudgingly, I picked up the spoon and lifted a bite to my mouth, even though my stomach was now in knots and I wasn't sure I could eat. Keeping my head down, I looked across the table from under my lashes. The man from the gallery was eating his soup and listening to the man next to him, a Black man in a black suit with an accent I couldn't place, but his eyes were on me. An emotion I couldn't name —or maybe I wasn't brave enough to try—put a crease between his brows as he studied me.

Then I felt the softest nudge against my foot under the table.

I ignored it, thinking it must have been an accident, but when I felt the gentle tap again, I chanced the briefest glance to my left, locking eyes with the man from the gallery. He gave me a small smile and moved his foot against mine. I had no idea what it meant, but the subtle contact made the rest of the meal more bearable.

Through the remaining courses, I tried to keep my head down, and the man across the table continued to stare, his foot still resting against mine. I'd tried valiantly to catch his name, but with the other conversations around the table and the clink and clatter of silverware on china, I hadn't been able to hear it if he'd said it at all. When the server reached for my plate following the final course, she leaned in and whispered, "Mr. Dasselaar would like you to remain here until all his guests have left the room."

I didn't acknowledge her request, but I sat back in my chair with my hands in my lap, trying to make myself inconspicuous. If I'd been able to shift, I would have been able to seamlessly blend into the background. Dasselaar wouldn't have been able to see me at all, or I could have taken my chameleon form and slipped from the room and the estate entirely, but with the drugs in my system, that was a dream I couldn't realize.

Dasselaar stood. "Please join me in the salon for an after-dinner drink and cigar if you're so inclined." His guests all stood. Everyone except the man from the gallery, who seemed to be stalling for time, swirling the last of his wine in the cut-crystal glass.

"Mr. Hunter, please join us."

I lifted my face to look at him, grateful to finally have a piece of a name. His eyes met mine again and he smiled, though the crease between his brows didn't go away. He brought his glass to his lips and drained the last of the deep red liquid. When his tongue slid between his lips to capture an errant drop, I felt my cock twitch. Every fantasy I'd ever had about *Mr. Hunter* rushed through my mind, and my hands tingled with warmth. Did the iridescent glow around my hands have something to do with him? And if so, what did he have to do with the painting?

He tapped my foot with his, then slowly slid it away and stood. I watched him go, knowing Dasselaar was standing near the door, his eyes on both of us. As he passed Dasselaar, he looked over his shoulder at me and gave me a small nod. I had no idea how to interpret the gesture, but it made me feel warm and safe for the first time since I'd become indentured to Stefan Dasselaar.

A small seed of something that felt like hope bloomed low in my belly, and I bit my cheek to keep from allowing a smile to spread across my face as I watched Mr. Hunter walk out of the room.

CHAPTER EIGHT

QUIN

THROUGHOUT DINNER, I'd tried to catch Dimitri's eyes, but he kept them downcast, and when the first server issued the reminder that Dimitri was supposed to behave like furniture, it had taken every ounce of willpower I had not to circle the table and pull him up out of his seat and into my arms. But that wouldn't have gone over well. So I'd watched him while the man seated next to me tried to engage me in conversation. I'd participated as little as possible, choosing to study Dimitri instead. He was beautiful, his face the perfect combination of soft curves and sharp lines that drew the eye to take in the whole picture. He ate carefully, almost like he didn't want to, and I found myself wondering if that was because he didn't like the food or didn't want to give Dasselaar the satisfaction of enjoying it. I was almost jealous of his spoon and fork as his mouth wrapped around them, and while the movement of his full lips was completely innocent, my mind wandered into fantasies of how those lips would feel against my skin, which made my pants uncomfortably tight.

But there was more to Dimitri than his physical beauty, and as I watched I saw his strength. I noticed the way his jaw clenched and his fingers tightened around his cutlery every time one of the servers delivered a thinly veiled threat on Dasselaar's behalf, and since I couldn't tear my eyes away from him, it was impossible to miss the resigned slump of his shoulders when the fleeting moment of anger passed. I could sense Dimitri wasn't used to being under someone's thumb and that he hated it, but he didn't feel like he had a choice other than to do whatever Dasselaar said.

I was desperate to give him a choice, to show him an option that had nothing to do with Stefan Dasselaar, but to make that happen, I had to know why he continued to stay. I needed to talk to him, but every time I opened my mouth to speak to him, another server issued another warning, and I bit back the words. The last thing I wanted was to get Dimitri in trouble or to tip my hand that I was paying close attention to him. I didn't need another reason to rouse Dasselaar's suspicions about my presence in Amsterdam, but by the end of the five-course meal, I couldn't take any more of Dimitri's silence.

So I'd lingered, hoping to get a chance to exchange a few words with the man who'd stolen my heart with a single glance, the man who fate had decided was mine.

Until Dasselaar kicked me out.

Instead of crossing the grand foyer of Dasselaar's imposing home and heading into the salon, I tucked myself into the shadows, waiting for Dimitri and Dasselaar to emerge from the dining room.

Dasselaar entered the foyer first, Dimitri, flanked by two heavily muscled bodyguards, following.

"You will be ready early tomorrow morning. You will be expected to wait in the auction room until the preview begins and then you will show my guests that each painting I am offering is authentic. You will not speak to anyone. Do I make myself clear?"

For a split second, I saw rage flash in Dimitri's bright green eyes, but he banked it quickly. He nodded.

"Janssen, take Dimitri back to his room, then you are dismissed for the evening."

The bodyguard standing on Dimitri's right, the one with the large scar marring his face who had watched Dimitri all through dinner, nodded. "Yes, Mr. Dasselaar." He grabbed Dimitri's arm as Dasselaar turned away from them and crossed the foyer to the salon.

I waited in my hiding spot until Janssen, Dimitri, and the other bodyguard reached the first landing and continued up the stairs instead of following the gallery to where Dasselaar's guests had been given rooms. After I'd arrived, I'd spent time wandering the floor where my room was located, and I'd found a second set of stairs that led up and down. Pretending I was returning to my room, I ducked down the second-floor hall and hustled to the rear staircase, climbing the steps as quickly as I could.

It was darker at this end of the hall, and the hidden staircase was lit only by ambient light coming in through the windows from lamps outside. When I reached the third floor, I stayed hidden at the top of the staircase and watched as one of the guards shoved Dimitri into a room at the far end of the hall. The bodyguard pulled the door closed, and I saw the glint of light on shiny metal as he locked the door from the outside, leaving Dimitri trapped inside.

In a rush, things suddenly made sense.

I'd wondered before why Dimitri let Dasselaar treat him the way he had at the gallery, but now I understood. Dimitri wasn't a colleague or an employee he was attempting to control. Dasselaar was keeping him under lock and key, and I needed to know why.

Making a mental note of which room was Dimitri's, I snuck back down the back stairs and into the room I'd been given for the weekend. In addition to the camera currently pinned to my lapel and the comm device still in my bag, Felix had given me a handheld device used to sweep for listening devices. I'd used it around the room when I arrived and hadn't found anything, but out of an abundance of caution, I pulled it from my bag again and scanned the room. The device stayed silent, and I tucked it away and pulled my cell phone out of my pocket, tapping Cal's contact as I lifted the phone to my ear.

Cal picked up on the second ring. "Quin. Is everything okay?"

"Dasselaar is holding Dimitri prisoner."

"Wait. What?"

"He's got him locked in a room."

"Fuck." Cal was quiet for a second, and I heard Jack in the background asking what was wrong, but my twin ignored him. "Poor kid. I swear we had no idea. Jack and I thought maybe he was blackmailing him or something. Do you think you can find out why Dasselaar has him locked up?"

"Dasselaar won't let him talk to anyone, but I have an idea."

My skills with a lockpick set were a little rusty, but I had to hope it was like riding a bike and the second I started trying to get into Dimitri's room the skills would snap back into place.

"Don't do anything stupid." Coming from Cal, the king of doing stupid things, that made me laugh.

"How about I won't do anything you wouldn't do?"

"Quin..."

"Cal..."

"You're not going to listen to me are you?" Cal sounded exasperated, and for a second I felt a little vindicated that he was finally getting the tiniest taste of what it was like to deal with him.

"Would you hold back if it was Jack?"

"You know I wouldn't. Just be careful, okay?"

"I promise."

"Let me know what you find out."

"I will. Can I talk to Felix for a second?"

"Uh, sure."

There was rustling on the other end of the line, then Felix's voice. "What can I do for you, Quin?"

"Are you able to loop the feeds on Dasselaar's cameras?"

He scoffed. "Is Batman Bruce Wayne?"

Felix was a little bit of a comic book nerd, and I didn't always understand all his references, but given his tone, I figured my question had been a dumb one. "Um, okay. I'm going to do some digging tonight. Do you think you can loop the feed for an hour or so?"

"Obviously."

"Perfect. I need to wait for things to die down here a little, so I'll text you when I'm ready to go."

"Sounds good. Cal bought me a case of these really awesome Dutch energy drinks, so I'll be up."

"Okay." I wasn't sure if that was a good thing or a bad thing.

"Hey, Quin?"

"Yeah?"

"Wear the comm. I'll watch the feeds for you. And I agree with Cal. Be careful. "

"I will. I'll text you." I disconnected the call before anyone else could issue another warning.

A glance at my watch told me I'd been gone from the party for too long. Slipping into the en suite bathroom, I freshened up a little bit, then went down the main staircase and into the salon. Everyone had a drink, and our host and several other men were out on the veranda enjoying a cigar.

Trying to make it look like I had been there the whole time, I made my way to the bar where a number of offerings had been laid out, including a bottle of green chartreuse that immediately reminded me of Dimitri's eyes. I ran my fingers over the bottle, turning it so it caught the light as I imagined Dimitri's eyes doing the same. I was tempted to tip a measure into my glass, but opted for a rare French cognac instead.

I moved from group to group, noticing that regardless of who I was speaking to, Dasselaar's gaze continuously found me. If I hadn't already assumed he'd invited me to his estate as a way to keep an eye on me, I would have guessed it now. I lingered in the room until the other guests began retiring to their rooms. When only the gentlemen still smoking on the veranda remained, I set my empty glass on the bar and started toward the door.

Dasselaar's voice stopped me in my tracks. "Mr. Hunter?"

Taking a breath, I turned around. "Thank you for your hospitality this evening."

He nodded. "I hope you are making the connections you were seeking."

"I am. Thank you again for the invitation."

"Of course." His tone was genial, but his face told me he wasn't convinced my motives were legitimate. Considering I was about to go upstairs and pull out my lockpick set while I waited for the house to quiet down, he had reason to be cautious.

"If you'll excuse me. I'm quite tired. I believe jet lag is finally catching up with me."

"Of course. I won't keep you any longer."

But I felt his eyes on me until I was out of the room.

My room overlooked the veranda below, which meant I had a front-row seat as several of Dasselaar's guests drank his alcohol and smoked his cigars into the small hours of the morning. Finally, the last of the men retired to his room, the house going quiet as he closed his door.

Grabbing my phone, I tapped out a quick text to Felix, letting him know it was time to kill the cameras. He sent back a thumbs-up emoji a few minutes later, signaling I was good to go. I flipped open the little leather box holding the ring and popped the tiny earpiece out, setting it into place in my ear.

"Hey, there." Felix's voice echoed in my ear.

"Hey. Everything ready to go?"

"Yep." I'll keep watch and let you know if I see anything on the real feeds."

"Thanks."

"No problem."

I waited for another five minutes, then slowly opened the door to my room. I'd changed into a black shirt and black athletic pants that could pass for pajamas if I got caught wandering around. In the dark, Felix's camera wasn't useful for helping to map out the interior of the estate, so I'd removed it from my lapel and set it in the box to charge. I slid my phone into one pocket and my small lockpick set into the other, then I stepped out into the hall. The house was dark and silent as I crept along the plush carpet toward the rear staircase. My heart hammered against my ribs, but I wasn't sure if that was because I was sneaking around in the dark without knowing if Dasselaar had guards patrolling the house at night or if I was just excited about the idea of seeing Dimitri again. I wanted to run up the stairs and straight to his door, but I held myself back, forcing myself to take it one step at a time and listening before I made a move.

On the third floor, I counted the doors until I found the only one locked from the outside. Kneeling in front of it, I pulled out my lockpick set and got to work. As I'd hoped, the second I had the pick in the lock, my hands moved without thought, feeling for tension on the pins like I had a million times before. The silence made it easier to visualize the inside of the lock, and in minutes, the pins gave, and the door unlocked.

I paused, barely breathing, listening intently for any indication that someone had heard me. When I heard nothing, I slowly turned the knob.

CHAPTER NINE

DIMITRI

SCRAPING in the lock on my door pulled me from another nightmare, and I sat bolt upright in bed, clutching the duvet to my naked chest. For a heartbeat, I thought maybe I'd dreamed the noise, that it had all been in my head, but terror climbed up my throat as I watched the knob turn and the door slowly start to swing open.

Dasselaar's men never came to my room at night, but Scar had been particularly handsy as he'd thrown me back into my room after dinner, and I wondered if tonight was the night his leers turned into something more sinister.

I had nowhere to run, so I sat frozen with fear, my heartbeat drowning out all other sounds as blood pounded in my ears dumping adrenaline into my veins, as a figure I didn't recognize stepped into my room and quietly closed the door.

"Wh-who's there?" I wasn't proud of the way my voice shook, but it was difficult to speak around the panic rising in my chest.

"It's Quin. Quin Hunter. I didn't mean to scare you. I promise I'm not here to hurt you."

Mr. Hunter. Mr. Hunter was in my room.

Why?

My fingers warmed, and for some reason, that settled the fear that had been threatening to overwhelm me. My heart rate slowed and my body relaxed, and when I looked down at my hands, the iridescent glow was visible even in the darkness. I reached for the lamp on my bedside table, and when the bulb flicked to life, I saw Mr. Hunter was still standing by the door. He'd made no attempt to come farther into the room, and that helped to dispel the rest of my panic.

"What are you doing here, Mr. Hunter?" Maybe the question was rude, but since he'd invaded my space, I felt like I was owed an answer.

"Please call me Quin." He shifted on his feet but didn't move, though it seemed like he wanted to. "As for what I'm doing in your room, I needed to talk to you, and it seems Dasselaar is doing his best to keep that from happening."

"How did you know where to find me?"

"I followed Dasselaar's men after he told them to take you back to your room. I saw them lock you in." Quin's brow creased with anger, the same way it had when Dasselaar had demanded I show him the Renoir in the gallery was real. His hands were balled into fists at his sides. He took a small step toward where I still sat in my bed, and I held my breath, waiting to see if he was going to come closer, but he didn't close the distance between us. "I don't like the way Dasselaar treats you."

My heart flipped over in my chest. I couldn't remember

the last time someone besides Athina had cared about me. Still, a scoff escaped my lips. "That makes two of us."

"Then why do you let him use you?" Quin looked honestly distressed, then upset that he'd asked the question. He shook his head. "That's not my business. I'm sorry I asked."

"I don't *let* him do anything."

Quin raised an eyebrow like he wanted me to elaborate, but regardless of how many times I'd drawn his face in my sketchbook or dreamed about being held in his arms, this was the first time we'd spoken. And even though he looked better in real life than he did in my head or in charcoal on paper, and my gut said I could trust him, it was too soon to lay all my vulnerabilities on the table just in case my instincts were wrong. Instead, I looked down at my hands, which continued to tingle with warmth. The glow around my fingers was brighter than ever, so I tucked my hands out of sight under the duvet, then changed the subject. "Do you have a brother?"

He narrowed his eyes, clearly confused by the question. "Yes. Three of them. Why do you ask?"

I wanted to reach for my sketchbook to show him the original picture I'd drawn, but I didn't, not ready to give that away yet either. "Does one of them look like you?"

He studied me carefully, much the way he had during dinner, and I got the distinct feeling he was seeing more than I wanted to reveal. "Yes. I have a twin."

"I think I've met him."

Quin nodded. "I know. He told me."

I waited for him to say more, but he didn't, even though his gaze continued to roam over me with such intensity it gave me goose bumps and sent a pleasant shiver down my spine that landed in my balls. Wanting this strange interaction, whatever it was, to last, I pivoted back to our previous topic, steering clear of my reasons for being Dasselaar's good little toy. "I find it hard to believe you went through the trouble of breaking into my room just to tell me you think Dasselaar is an asshole."

Quin took a tiny step forward, and my pulse picked up, not because I was afraid but because I was hoping he would finally come closer. Sitting up against the headboard, I shifted on the bed to make room for him. The duvet dropped away from my naked torso, and I felt Quin's gaze fall to my chest, studying it like he would need to paint me from memory. When his eyes found mine in the dimly lit room, there was a hint of fire in his dark irises, and a thrill of desire unfurled in my core.

When he didn't move closer to the bed, I pulled my hand from under the duvet and patted the space I'd made for him, trying to ignore the fact that I had decided to sleep in the nude and had nothing on under the blanket.

He still didn't take the hint.

"Please sit. You're making me nervous."

"I'm sorry. I'm screwing this up so badly."

"Why don't we start over?" From my position on the bed, I held out my hand. "I'm Dimitri Chrysanthos." Quin studied my hand for so long I thought he might not shake it. I started to pull it back, but he grabbed my fingers, and the second our palms touched, it felt like I'd brushed a live wire. Tingling heat moved from where our hands met up through my body until it felt like he was touching me everywhere from the inside out. Maybe I'd been alone and starved for gentle touch for too long, but I never wanted to let Quin's warm, callused hand go.

Unless it was so he could touch me somewhere less innocent.

Quin gasped, and his eyes met mine, the tiny fire that had been simmering there now a roaring inferno, and I was pleased to see I wasn't the only one instantly affected by our connection.

He might not have been there to hurt me, but there was no denying Quin Hunter was dangerous.

To my heart.

Quin looked down at where our hands were joined, then up at me, a look of awe on his face as though he was feeling what I was feeling. "I'm Quin Hunter."

Reluctantly, I let go of his hand, my fingers still buzzing from his touch. "It's a pleasure to meet you, Quin Hunter. What brings you to my room at this time of night?" I patted the spot on my bed again, and Quin finally sat. He held himself stiffly, like he was afraid to relax.

"I'm here because I need your help."

That surprised me. "My help? Why do you need my help?"

Quin answered my question with a question of his own. "How long have you been living here?"

I thought *living* was a generous way to describe what I'd been doing. *Existing* felt more appropriate, but I understood what he meant. "Over a year."

"A year?" His hands balled into fists again where they rested against his thighs, his anger palpable. "He's kept you locked up here for a year?"

"He lets me out for meals and when he needs me at the gallery or at one of his meetings."

The muscle in Quin's jaw ticked. "That's unacceptable."

"There's nothing I can do about it for now, so why don't you tell me what it is you need me to do for you."

His gaze swept over my features, and he shook his head, then mumbled like he was talking to himself and pulled something from his ear, closing his fist around it so I couldn't see what he held. "My brothers are going to kill me. This is why I don't do fieldwork." He rubbed a hand over his face. "Do you want to be here, Dimitri?"

Quin's question took me aback. The answer was obvious. "Do I want to be locked away, drugged, and at Dasselaar's beck and call? No, Quin. I'm pretty sure I'd rather be anywhere else."

"Drugged? What do you mean?" His words came out through clenched teeth.

Sighing, I gave Quin a tiny piece of my story, hoping like hell that I could trust my intuition about him. "I'm a chameleon shifter." Quin's eyes went wide. "When Dasselaar saw what I could do, like what I did with the Renoir and the forged Vermeer at his gallery, he made me an offer I couldn't refuse. Because chameleon shifters can change their appearance at will, we are bound to the countries we are born in unless we're granted permission to leave by our country's government or we leave the country illegally. I chose the latter when I left Cyprus. Dasselaar found out and has used that information to his advantage. Since I'm small in my shifted form, almost the size of one of my wild cousins, Dasselaar couldn't allow me to shift because that would mean I could take my animal form and slip through his grasp. He keeps me on a steady dose of antitransmutative drugs that allow me to partially shift so I can do what he wants but makes it so I can't shift beyond that."

By the time I finished speaking, Quin's fists were so tight his knuckles had gone white. "You haven't shifted in over a year?"

I shook my head.

"I'm going to kill him."

Quin's vehement response on my behalf made me feel warm in a way that even his touch hadn't. "Is that what you need my help with?"

Almost like he'd forgotten what we'd been talking about, he shook his head, then looked at me with softness in his previously tense features. "No. I would never put you at risk like that."

Little did Quin know my life was at risk every day, whether I planned on attempting to take Dasselaar's life or not.

"So then, what do you need me for?"

"My grandmother is Juno Hunter, a famous art thief. My brothers and I are here because we think one of the paintings Dasselaar is going to auction off is part of a bigger plot that involves my family. We think Dasselaar has invited whoever is targeting my family to the gala."

"Okay." I wasn't sure what any of that could possibly have to do with me.

"I need to find the guest list and any information Dasselaar is holding on to about the painting so my brothers can start doing research." Quin looked at me seriously. "I hate to ask you for this, but is there any way you could take me to Dasselaar's study or office? We weren't able to get the list from any of the computers at the gallery."

"That's because he hates technology. He doesn't trust it. He thinks it's too easy to manipulate, and a digital footprint is forever. You can't just kill it to make it go away." A shudder shivered down my spine as my mind conjured up an image of the truck driver lying in a pool of cooling blood, and I had to close my eyes to push the memory away.

Quin nodded. "Oddly, that makes sense. I looked into the transactions for the gallery and none of the bills of lading have been filed electronically."

"Like I said, I'm not free to roam the estate. I've only been to Dasselaar's study here a few times, but I think I remember where it is."

"Will you show me?" Quin's eyes were pleading.

The thought of wandering around Dasselaar's estate in the middle of the night was oddly thrilling. It was a type of freedom I hadn't tasted in a long, long time, and if we were going to break into Dasselaar's study, I could look for anything I could possibly use to free myself and my sister while Quin looked for his list.

"Yes."

CHAPTER TEN

QUIN

THE SECOND I walked into Dimitri's room, everything changed for me. This op was no longer about the painting or Juno or even Felix. For me, it was only about Dimitri. The more he told me about the way Dasselaar treated him, the more rage burned through my blood, obliterating any of my previous plans and replacing them with one singular mission.

To keep Dimitri safe.

And the only way to do that was to get him as far away from Stefan Dasselaar as possible.

"If I'm going to help you, I need to get dressed." Dimitri started to push the blanket away, and I stood, offering him a hand to help him up. He smiled up at me but didn't take my hand. For a second I wondered if it was because he didn't want to feel the connection between us again. My skin still hummed where we'd touched, and I ached to feel the sensation anew. "I, uh, sleep in the nude, so, I, um, need you to turn around."

Without my permission, my gaze slid over his naked

chest and down to where his smooth bronze flesh disappeared under the duvet. He'd been naked this whole time? Why did that turn me on? Shaking my head, I forced my eyes to meet Dimitri's again. He was smirking and raised a finger in the air, making a circling motion.

"Oh, right." I stepped away from the bed and turned around, listening as he climbed out of bed and crossed the room to the large chest of drawers between the windows, sliding one of the drawers open.

Despite our circumstances, the electric heat of Dimitri's touch still burned in my veins, and I couldn't keep my mind from conjuring up images of what he'd look like naked. I pictured his smooth skin stretched over a sweet, round ass and long, lean legs, that I knew would feel amazing wrapped around my body as I slid deep inside him. My mouth would find his and his plush lips would taste so sweet I'd be instantly addicted. I would get lost in him for hours, and when I was done taking him apart and his pupils were blown wide in his brilliant green eyes, I would draw him sprawled out beneath me, ecstasy on his face.

Dimitri cleared his throat like he'd tried to get my attention more than once. The fantasy was so vivid, I'd forgotten for a second where I was. When I turned to face Dimitri, his eyes immediately fell to my cock, which was more than half hard beneath the black tactical pants I'd borrowed from Cal.

Embarrassed by my lack of self-control, I ignored Dimitri's hungry gaze and pushed forward with my plan.

"My brother's mate is looping the camera feeds, but we don't have much time. Are you ready?"

Dimitri nodded. He'd put on a black long-sleeved T-shirt and black jeans, and I wanted to strip him bare, to see his golden skin again. I wished more than anything that he wasn't involved in this at all, but the only way I could get him out was to get the information we needed and hopefully find something else we could use as a bargaining chip to get Dimitri out from under Dasselaar's control.

Dimitri nodded. "It feels weird to be leaving the room without one of Dasselaar's goons."

Rage simmered low in my belly, but I pushed it away, attempting to focus on what we needed to do. "I promise it won't be the last."

Dimitri smiled but it faded quickly, and I watched him war with something before locking his emotions down and smiling again. "Okay."

I wasn't sure what that meant, but we were wasting time, and we needed to get to Dasselaar's office. I settled the comm device back in my ear and immediately heard Felix on the other end.

"Quin? Thank fuck. Nero was losing his shit."

"Sorry."

Felix chuckled. "No, I get it. You needed to have a private conversation. Just do me a favor and maybe don't do that again."

"Sorry."

Dimitri was watching me, clearly confused, so I pointed at my ear. "Felix. He's running comms and watching the cameras for me."

He nodded and took another step toward the door. I followed, and reaching out, I turned the doorknob and peeked out into the silent hall.

"Clear on my end," Felix said in my ear.

"It's clear. Lead the way."

Dimitri stepped over the threshold and took a deep breath like he was tasting his freedom, then he looked up and down the hall like he was trying to decide which way to go while I relocked the door.

"This way." He pointed to the right, toward the rear staircase, and we made our way in that direction on nearly silent feet, the plush antique rugs along the hall muffling our footsteps.

Dimitri took the stairs all the way to the ground level, then paused and once again considered where he was in the house. "I'm pretty sure it's this way." He pointed to the left. I knew from my walkaround earlier that the dining room, salon, and foyer were that way, but I nodded and followed Dimitri.

All the rooms were dark, and the halls were lit by sconces that had been turned down low, creating long shadows along each corridor.

"You're clear." Felix's voice made me jump and my heart race more than it already had been. "I don't see anyone up and about right now, so it should be smooth sailing." I wanted to tell him those sounded an awful lot like famous last words, but I didn't dare make a sound.

Dimitri instinctively stuck to the shadows, and I followed him down the hall past the dining room. Once we passed the dining room, the hallway opened up and became a gallery with windows that looked out over the circular front drive. Moonlight lit the hall, making the shadows harder to come by, and I stepped up alongside Dimitri, blocking him from the windows, just in case someone was outside and saw us moving through the house. I believed Felix when he said he didn't see anyone wandering the estate, but I didn't want to take a chance. I could blame curiosity and insomnia for why I was up prowling around Dasselaar's home if caught, but that wouldn't explain Dimitri's presence.

"It's this way," Dimitri whispered low and pointed to the right.

We turned down another hallway and moved past a conservatory. The walls and ceiling were glass, and potted trees lined the space. Other plants were positioned in tall iron holders, long vines spilling over the edges until they almost brushed the floor. Two low white couches sat in the middle of the room facing each other with a marble coffee table in between. During the day, the space was probably lovely, but now, bathed in blue light from the moon, it looked otherworldly, the leaves of the plants caught in shadows that stretched unnaturally across the floor.

At the turn in the hallway, there was a set of dark wood double doors, and Dimitri walked up to them and tried the doorknob but it didn't turn. "It's locked."

I fumbled in the pocket of my borrowed tactical pants and produced my lockpick set. "Not a problem."

Dimitri stepped back, and I knelt in front of the door.

"Do you need a light?"

I shook my head. "No. There's nothing to see, and I can do this by feel." I found the pins and adjusted my pressure until the lock clicked and the door swung in, the hinges creaking slightly.

Dimitri and I both froze, the small sound feeling too loud in the silent stillness of the house.

"You're still good." Felix's reassuring voice in my ear made me release the breath I was holding.

"Thanks, Felix."

Dimitri stepped into the room, and I followed. Ambient light from outside filtered into the room from floor-to-ceiling windows bracketing a stone hearth on the far wall. Books lined the room-height shelves, and a large leather sofa and two wingback chairs were positioned in the center of the room just in front of the fireplace.

"I've only been in here twice, but I wish Dasselaar would let me at least visit this room." The longing in Dimitri's voice was almost tangible, and I mentally promised myself we would get him out of here. We had to. There was no other acceptable option. He was mine, and he would be coming home with me. No matter what.

"Do you like to read?"

"I do, but the light in here is beautiful, and I'd love to be able to lounge in front of a roaring fire and sketch."

"You draw?"

"And paint and sculpt, though I haven't had the chance to do much of either over the past year. Dasselaar would only give me a sketchbook and drawing pencils."

"We're going to get you out of here, and I will make sure you have every art supply you could ever want."

"What is your favorite medium?"

His question brought me up short. "What makes you think I'm an artist?"

"I've seen your hands." I looked down at them, but in the dark I couldn't make out the imperfections I knew were there. "Only an artist has stains and calluses like that on their hands."

While I kept my hands as clean and neatly manicured as possible, Dimitri was right, there were certain things that couldn't be hidden as much as I tried. Years of crafting and working with pigment-based oil paints had left their mark in the form of stains I could no longer remove no matter how hard I scrubbed. Long-healed scars earned from carving up blocks of marble crisscrossed my palms, and calluses had formed from hours of wielding paintbrushes and other tools.

"I like to paint."

Dimitri hummed like that was the answer he was expecting and moved farther into the room. He disappeared into a small alcove between two bookcases, then poked his head out. "This is Dasselaar's study. The door here is locked too."

He stepped out of the alcove completely, and I stepped in, removing my lockpick set and getting to work. This lock was more complicated and more difficult to open than the one on Dimitri's door or the one to the library, and it took me longer than it should have to understand the placement of the pins. Sweat beaded on my brow. I knew in my gut that some of our answers lay on the other side of the door, and the pressure to open the lock and find the information that might be able to help us set Dimitri free bore down on me.

A cool hand touched the back of my neck, making me freeze even as heat emanated from the spot and sent my blood rushing south. It was an innocent touch, but the slide of Dimitri's elegant fingers against the back of my neck was almost as arousing as if he'd been stroking his hand over my cock. He kneaded the muscles where my neck met my shoulders, and the self-induced tension seeped from my bones.

"Relax, Quin. You can do this." His hand slid down my arm, his long fingers wrapping around my wrist. His words brushed the shell of my ear, making me shiver.

I took a deep breath, feeling for the pins in the lock again, and this time, I was able to get the tension just right. The lock gave, and I turned the knob, opening the door to Dasselaar's private study. "Thank you." I turned over my shoulder to find Dimitri's face only inches from mine. His full lips were tipped up in a soft smile, and I wanted to close the tiny distance between us and lock our mouths together. His tongue peeked out and swiped across his lower lip before he bit down on it with his top teeth.

Without thought, I reached out and pulled the soft flesh free. Dimitri's mouth fell open, inviting me to kiss him, and I was moving forward, closing the distance between us when Felix's voice in my ear snapped me back to the present.

"What's happening? It's really quiet. Quin? Are you still there?"

I sighed, pulling myself back from the brink of kissing Dimitri. "Yes. I'm still here. I just got the door to Dasselaar's study open."

"Okay. Good. A light just went on in the second-floor hallway, so you might want to hurry."

"Got it." Turning to Dimitri, I tipped my head toward the office. "Let's go."

"What are we looking for again?"

I rattled off the list Nero had made me memorize. "Guest list, guard count and schedule, security schematics for the auction." I added *anything we can use as leverage to get Dimitri out* to the list.

"Got it."

Inside Dasselaar's study, we went separate ways. Dimitri started looking through the built-in shelves and drawers while I took the desk. Unlike his desk at the gallery, which had been neat and uncluttered, Dasselaar's desk at the estate was covered with file folders and papers. I started at the top of one pile, being careful to keep everything exactly as it was. The first few papers were shipping manifests. As Cal and Jack had assumed, he'd run the items for the auction into the gallery instead of having them brought directly to his estate. At first, I thought moving the paintings twice was stupid, but if any crew interested in stealing from Dasselaar had access to his home, they would have access to everything he had at the estate. Letting everything come to the gallery and then trickle out to his estate meant anyone who thought they were going to hit a big score by taking out one of the trucks moving between the gallery and the estate would be sorely disappointed since he moved a painting at a time, all on different routes. It was either incredibly inefficient or some sort of genius.

But it wasn't overly helpful at this point.

Carefully, I moved that stack of papers aside. A hint of blue caught my eye, and I moved several file folders to unearth the blue folder. Ilse had brought in a similar folder when Dasselaar had asked for the guest list during our meeting and I crossed my fingers that this was it. Flipping it open, I let out a breath.

"Found the guest list."

Dimitri jumped at the sound of my voice but recovered

quickly and came to look over my shoulder. "I recognize a few of the names. Dasselaar has done business with some of these people in the past."

"That's good to know. As Felix and my brother Julius dig into this, they might have questions."

"I don't know much, but I'll help however I can."

"Thank you." Pulling out my phone, I took a picture and sent it to Felix. The list was completely handwritten, which explained why Felix and Julius had been unable to find it on Dasselaar's computer and further supported Nero's claim that he would rather rely on people than technology for his security.

I worked through each page, mentally tallying two hundred and fifty names. On the last page, a note written to the side in a different pen caught my eye.

Quin Hunter. Security concern?

My instinct that Dasselaar was suspicious of me had been spot on. Not that it mattered. He'd let me into his house, despite those suspicions, and now I had one piece of the information we needed.

I slid the folder back where I'd found it, and Dimitri continued to go through the drawers.

"I think I found something." He held a drawer open and gestured for me to come over.

"What is it?"

"Looks like a ledger. I can't really tell if it's useful or not."

In the drawer was a large leatherbound book. Dimitri had it open to the first page where a list of debits and credits dated this week were listed. Several of the debits were for ten thousand dollars apiece to a list of thirty individual names. "These could be the added security personnel for the gala."

"I'm not sure. I can tell you there are ten different men who have been in charge of drugging me and moving me where Dasselaar wants me. I don't know any of their names to be able to tell you if they are on this list."

"That's okay. Between Felix and my brother, they'll figure it out." I snapped a picture and sent it off, then flipped through a few more of the ledger's pages and sent those over too.

Felix had been quiet in my ear, and I wondered if I'd gotten disconnected from him or if he was already working on combing through the guest list.

We worked for a little while longer, going through everything we could find, but all I'd found that was helpful after the guest list and the ledger had been the schematics for some concealed pressure sensor alarms. I figured Dasselaar would be using those in the auction room to make sure no one tried to walk away with a painting. I hadn't found anything incriminating we could use against Dasselaar, and I was beginning to think we were going to have to break Dimitri out the old-fashioned way with a smash-and-grab.

"Let's go. I don't think we're going to find anything else."

Dimitri had his back to me, a manilla file folder in his hand. He didn't turn around when I spoke to him, so I moved to stand next to him, reading over his shoulder.

"Who is Athina?"

Dimitri jumped like he didn't know I was standing there. "Uh, no one." He dropped the file back into the drawer and closed it. "Are you done?"

"I think so." I tipped my head toward the drawer he'd just shut. "Are you?"

"What?" He shook his head. "Oh, yeah. I'm good."

But he didn't look good. He looked rattled. And I wanted to know what was in that file. But we'd already pressed our luck long enough.

"Let's get out of here."

CHAPTER ELEVEN

DIMITRI

QUIN WORKED FAST, relocking Dasselaar's office door and the door to the library while my mind spun through what I'd seen in that file in Dasselaar's office. It was stupid to think he wasn't keeping a file on me and Athina, but I hadn't realized he'd already made plans for when I was no longer useful to him. His notes said that upon my untimely death, Athina was going to be sent back to Cyprus with nothing. If that happened, she would be immediately arrested for leaving the country illegally and put in jail.

The thought of my baby sister rotting away in some jail cell without the proper medical care for her condition made me physically sick, especially since I wouldn't be around anymore to do anything about it. I was more upset about her fate than I was about my own, but seeing that file made me certain of one thing.

I was going to need to tell Quin about Athina.

He seemed determined to make sure I got out from under Dasselaar, and I had to hope and pray he'd extend the same offer to Athina.

Quin shoved me hard against the wall in front of the conservatory, his hand covering my mouth when I started to ask what was happening.

"Shh. I hear something."

I held my breath, listening hard. Quin was right. I heard voices and they were getting louder coming this way.

"Felix," Quin hissed under his breath, but I could tell from his facial expression that Felix didn't respond. "Shit." He looked around, then tugged me into the conservatory and into the shadows against one of the only solid walls in the room, his wider body blanketing mine.

My face was tucked into his neck, and I pulled his scent deep into my lungs. He smelled so damn good—sea salt, and pine, and something a little minty. It reminded me of home, of crystal blue water and sunshine. The feel of his hard body against mine went straight to my head. He felt exactly like I thought he would, and even though it was one hundred percent not the right time, I couldn't keep my body from responding, my dick thickening behind the zipper of my jeans. With the way Quin was holding himself against me, there was no way he didn't notice.

Quin's hand was braced on the wall next to my head, and he leaned into me, dragging his nose along my neck, breathing me in like I was doing to him. His body pressed closer to mine, and I felt his arousal brush my thigh.

Thank god I wasn't in this alone.

Reaching up, I tangled my fingers in his hair and pulled his head up so he was looking at me.

"What—"

But I cut off his question by crashing my lips to his.

At first, his mouth was hard, but in a heartbeat, his lips molded to mine. A moan threatened to crawl up my throat, but I remembered where we were and what we were doing and I held it back. Quin's tongue teased across the seam of my lips, the slide of his silken tongue against me more than I was prepared for, and my mouth dropped open, giving him access that he took without a second of hesitation, his tongue licking into my mouth and tangling with mine as he deepened the kiss. I felt it in every cell of my body.

Quin's strong artist's fingers traced up my side, his hand firm against my body like he was mapping my form so he could sculpt it later, and I melted into the touch. It had been so long since I'd been touched like this, been kissed like this, that if Quin hadn't been holding me up against the wall I would have dissolved into a puddle at his feet.

He nudged my feet apart and slid a knee between my legs as he bit at my bottom lip, then soothed away the ache with his tongue. His hand came to rest at my hip and he gripped it tight, tugging me against him so I could rock my erection against his thigh, the friction perfect. My underwear was already sticky with precum, but I didn't care. This felt too good. It was all too good, and I was hurtling toward release with speed that would have embarrassed a teenager.

Quin's lips tugged at my earlobe, and a bolt of pleasure went straight to my cock, making it twitch. Sensing my reaction, Quin did it again and again until I was so close my vision was starting to go white around the edges. Having Quin in my arms, wrapped around my body and holding me close in his strong arms was better than any of the fantasies I'd made up to get me through the long lonely nights I spent locked up in my room.

But as quickly as it started, it was over.

Quin used his grip on my hip to hold me still, and when I started to protest, he covered my mouth with his, swallowing my words.

The voices were louder now, right beyond the wall where we were hiding, and we both went still, straining to hear what they were saying.

"What about the boy?" I recognized the voice as Scar's.

"After the gala, make sure he disappears. He's becoming a liability." That was Dasselaar. Bile rose in my throat. I'd known my days were numbered, but I thought I had more time to figure out a plan.

Scar said something I couldn't hear, and Dasselaar laughed, the cold sound sending a shiver down my spine. "If you want him, he's yours. Just make sure to get rid of him when you're done."

Keys jingled, and I heard the slight creak that indicated the library door had been opened. It creaked again and closed with a click before Quin pulled back.

"We need to get out of here. Is there another way back to your room?"

"Yes. I think so."

He ducked his head out into the hallway. Light was visible under the library doors, but the corridor was quiet. "Come on. We'll stick to the shadows."

Quin let me pass in front of him, and instead of going back the way we'd come, I led him down a hall that curved to the right past the library at the back of the house. Sometimes Dasselaar's goons brought me this way when they were taking me to the garage, and I said a silent prayer that the back stairs connected here somewhere. Quin spotted a staircase before I did and pushed me toward it. I stumbled on the first step, but he caught me, holding me up and helping me get steady on my feet.

"Are you okay?"

"I'm fine. I just don't really know where I am. I told you I didn't know the house well."

"It's okay. We'll figure it out."

This wasn't a staircase I had ever been on before, and trying to place it in the house had me all turned around. I didn't recognize anything on the first landing, and Quin tugged my hand, pulling me up the next flight of stairs. At the top of the next set of stairs, everything was in shadow. We came out in a little alcove off a main hall, and Quin glanced out into the corridor while I tried to get my bearings.

"Your room is over there. Stay here. I'm going to pick the lock. I'll come get you when I'm done." He shoved me back into the alcove and dropped a quick kiss to my forehead that had butterflies taking flight low in my belly.

Quin disappeared, and I stayed tucked into the shadows, counting the seconds and listening for any movement that wasn't Quin. My fingers started to tingle, and I glanced down to see the iridescent glow was back, so I shoved my hands into my pockets.

"Okay, your door is open and the coast is clear." Quin's voice made me jump, but I moved quickly into the hall. If Dasselaar and Scar were awake and wandering the estate, there was no telling who else might be prowling the halls.

The second we were in my room with the door shut

behind us, Quin shoved one of his lockpick tools into the doorknob. "If they try the door it will seem locked."

I nodded. My heart was trying to beat out of my chest as everything I'd read in Dasselaar's file on my sister and heard him say in the hall finally settled around me, and I started to shake.

Quin crossed the room and wrapped me in his embrace. "You're okay, Dimitri. You're okay. I promise. I promise I'm going to get you out of here and out of Amsterdam. I'm not going to let anything happen to you. I'll kill Dasselaar myself before I let him touch you."

It was so much more complicated than that, and while I knew I needed to tell him about Athina and beg him to help her too, I held back, letting his comforting touch soothe my frayed edges.

Quin's hands stroked over my back, and my breathing started to return to normal as I relaxed within his hold.

"You should try to get some more sleep." He whispered the words next to my ear, and I felt a little thrill shoot down my spine.

I nodded against his chest. "Will you stay with me?" I had no right to make the request. Quin was already putting himself in danger for the op he was trying to pull with his brothers. If he were caught with me, Dasselaar would probably just kill us both, but I still wanted him to say yes.

"Of course."

I pushed away from his chest to see his face and make sure he wasn't teasing me. "Really?"

"I don't think it's a good idea for me to stay all night, but I want to hold you until you fall asleep."

"Please." The word came out on a sob as I hoped Quin would somehow be able to hold my nightmares back.

"Get undressed, climb into bed, and tell me when you're ready." Quin turned around, giving me privacy, even though I really wanted him to watch. I wanted to see his reaction to my body almost as much as I wanted to feel his callused palms on my skin. But I'd already asked for enough tonight, and tomorrow I would need to ask for even more when I told him about my sister. For tonight, letting him hold me would be enough.

When I was naked, I climbed under the duvet and pulled it up around my chest. "I'm ready."

Quin turned around, double-checking that I was tucked in, and toed off his shoes, leaving them by the door. I watched him cross the room and position himself on the bed. He stayed on top of the duvet but reached over to pull me close, fitting me against his body with the blanket between us. One day, I would ask him to hold me like this with nothing separating us, not a blanket or his clothes, but for now, just having him here was enough. The warmth of his body and the comforting weight of his arm around me made my eyelids heavy.

I'd been wrong to think no one was coming to rescue me.

Quin was here, and he had every intention of getting me out.

Even if he failed, I could die happy knowing what it felt like to be held by him.

And it was enough.

CHAPTER TWELVE

QUIN

I SNUCK out of Dimitri's room as the sun started to rise. It almost hurt to leave him. But he was sleeping peacefully, so I tiptoed out and locked the door behind me.

Back in my own room, I called Felix. He answered on the second ring.

"Quin! Oh, thank god. What happened?"

"I don't know. You tell me. One minute you were there and the next, I had nothing. We had a close call."

"Shit. I'm sorry. Are you okay?"

I blew out a sigh as memories from last night scrolled through my brain. Dimitri had felt so perfect in my arms, his lips on mine. I could have done without almost getting caught sneaking around Dasselaar's estate, but I definitely didn't regret kissing Dimitri or holding him until he fell asleep. Recalling the sweet little sounds he'd made while he rubbed his cock against my thigh had my cock thickening behind my zipper.

The sound of frantic typing came over the line. "Where is the comm now?"

I picked up one of the leather cases and snapped the earpiece back into place. "I just put it back in the ring, and the ring is in the box."

"Good. Let me run some tests. Hopefully it was just a blip with the battery and charging it up will help."

"Did you get my texts?"

"Yes. Having the guest list is huge. Julius is already working on hacking bank accounts so we can monitor the money moving during the auction. I've been working with Reuben to pull profiles for all the attendees, and we're already about halfway through the list."

"When was the last time you slept?"

"Um, yesterday? Maybe. I don't remember. I'll get through a few more names then crash for a while."

"Dasselaar is doing a preview of the auction today, so I should be able to get some good information on the setup of the pieces and the layout of the room. Can you ask Jules if the account is good to go?"

"Julius says you're all set. I know Nero is getting nervous about going in blind, so anything you can get us of the inside of the estate helps. I have a program that will create a 3D rendering from the footage your camera picks up."

A yawn cracked my jaw. "Okay."

"Sounds like you need to get some sleep too."

"Yeah."

"Then I'll let you go. Text me if you need anything. If I'm sleeping, Nero will answer."

"Got it."

Julius said something to Felix, and he ended the call.

Still fully clothed, I flopped onto the bed and stared up

at the ceiling. All I could see were Dimitri's bright green eyes, his pupils blown from pleasure, his lips swollen from my kisses. His soft sounds played on a loop in my head, and I fell asleep thinking of him.

When I woke up, I had just enough time to quickly scroll through the profiles Felix had sent to me, grab a shower, change into a fresh suit, put Felix's pin camera into place on my pocket, and hustle down to breakfast. Only a couple of Dasselaar's guests lingered in the dining room, and I recognized both as two of the men who had stayed up until well past midnight drinking and smoking cigars on the veranda. As I picked up a plate to serve myself from the buffet spread, the door to the kitchen swung open, and I held my breath waiting to see if it was Dimitri.

It wasn't. A member of the kitchen staff came into the room carrying a silver coffee carafe. She set it down and hustled from the room.

I tucked into my breakfast at the far end of the table from where two gentlemen were deep in a hushed conversation. A bite of boiled egg was halfway to my mouth when the dining room door banged open, and Dasselaar strode in.

"Ah, Mr. Hunter. I wondered if we'd be seeing you today."

My fork fell back to the plate. "My apologies. I overslept a bit."

Dasselaar studied me, his gaze penetrating, and his lips tipped up in half of a sly smile. "I see. I thought perhaps you were up late."

His words put ice in my veins. Did he know Dimitri and I had broken into his office last night? He couldn't know.

Felix had been looping the cameras. But there had been that issue with the comms. What if something had knocked out Felix's feed?

Pulling on my cool, professional persona, I shook my head. "No. I went to bed after I saw you last night. I just had trouble getting to sleep."

"Mm." The single syllable conveyed Dasselaar's skepticism, but he didn't press the issue further, which made me think he was trying to see if I would give myself away rather than having any real proof of what Dimitri and I had been up to last night. Still, I didn't like that I was so clearly on his radar.

"I'm looking forward to the auction preview this afternoon." I lifted my fork again, and this time, Dasselaar let me take the bite.

"My team is making the final preparations now." Dasselaar pulled out the seat next to me and lowered himself into the chair. "I have made a request that all my guests make a deposit of a half million US dollars to secure their position at the auction. Before I can allow you into the preview, I will need your deposit."

"That's not a problem."

"My banker is here now and happy to meet with you as soon as you are ready."

Picking up my coffee, I took a sip and studied Dasselaar over the rim of the delicate cup. "Of course. Let me finish here, and I will be happy to meet him."

"Excellent. He will be waiting for you in the library." Dasselaar watched my face for any indication that I was already familiar with that part of the house.

"Where is the library located?"

Dasselaar was quiet for a moment, and I returned to my egg, waiting him out. "Follow the gallery to the first hall and make a right. It is the set of double doors at the end of that corridor." He looked at me intently again. "Right next to the conservatory."

Somehow he knew Dimitri had been out of his room and with me last night. That was the only reason he would be baiting me like this. But if he had proof, he would have had his security team take care of me, right? He certainly wouldn't be letting me sit in his dining room, casually eating a meal.

Until I knew for sure that he was aware Dimitri and I had been prowling the estate after hours, I had to remain cool and collected. "If I get turned around, I'm sure there are plenty of people I can ask to point me in the right direction."

Before Dasselaar could respond, a member of Dasselaar's security team walked into the dining room and straight to him, leaning down to whisper something I couldn't hear into his ear.

"If you'll excuse me, there is something that requires my attention."

"Don't let me keep you."

"I will let my banker know to expect you."

I nodded and Dasselaar stood, following his goon from the room.

After finishing my breakfast, I made my way to the library, moving slowly so the camera picked up as much as possible. I pretended to get lost, turning down the second hallway on the right instead of the first, then doubled back. I stopped along the way to admire some of the art Dasselaar had displayed on the walls. The only thing the pieces had in common were their rarity and their price points, but otherwise, there was no cohesive vision when it came to the collection. His taste reminded me of someone who ordered the most expensive thing on the menu at a restaurant just because it was the most expensive thing, not because they actually liked the meal.

Today, the double doors to the library were open and the sun streamed in through the floor-to-ceiling windows. Several of Dasselaar's guests were in the room. A lovely older Asian lady sat on one of the leather sofas in front of the fireplace, reading a leatherbound volume. I recognized her from Felix's files as Naga Tatsumi, a Komodo dragon shifter and owner of a string of high-end, luxury casinos from Macau to Singapore, including several properties in Las Vegas.

Sergei Lobanov—a wolf shifter and Russian general turned steel magnate—and Gareth Hawking—a falcon shifter and chemist who was one of the UK's wealthiest people—sat across from each other in leather club chairs, a chess board between them. From what I could tell, it was Lobanov's move.

"Mr. Hunter?" An accented voice caught my attention, and I turned to find a rotund man wearing a maroon paisley bow tie and round glasses that made his eyes look owlish and wide at a table just inside the door.

"Yes?"

"Mr. Dasselaar said I should be expecting you. I am Emil Mondvogel, Mr. Dasselaar's private banker. If you'll join me, we can complete your deposit."

I nodded and followed him to the table where a laptop sat.

"Do you have any Swiss bank accounts?" Mondvogel asked.

"I do, but I'd prefer to use a different account for this transaction."

"Of course. Of course. Whatever you prefer." He spun the laptop around. "This is a private and highly secure wire transfer program. You simply enter your details here." He tapped a field on the screen. "And I will enter Mr. Dasselaar's details below, then this panel will take your handprint, and the transaction will be complete."

I nodded my understanding, and Mondvogel gestured for me to proceed. I typed in the account numbers Julius had made me memorize for an off-shore account that couldn't be traced back to us. When I was done, Mondvogel turned the computer back to face him and typed in Dasselaar's details. The palm reader lit up red and Mondvogel pointed to it. "I simply need your handprint to complete the transaction. Place your hand flat and hold it still until the light turns green."

I did as he said, and within a second, the light flashed.

"Very well. That is done. If you are the highest bidder on a piece, you will just need to scan your palm again to authorize the transfer of funds for your purchase. Enjoy the auction."

As I left the library, the only thing I could think about was the fact that I would be leaving Dasselaar's auction with something far more valuable than a painting. I would be leaving with my mate. With my Dimitri.

I had time to kill before the preview, and I spent it

slowly walking around the estate, poking into every room I could find, and giving Felix as much of an overview of the inside of the estate as I could. While I was wandering, Julius sent me a text telling me the money had been swept out of the account and he'd been able to use the transaction to trace back into Dasselaar's accounts.

At noon, I made my way to the wing of the house where the ballroom was located and stood at the back of the group of Dasselaar's guests who had gathered for the preview. While I'd been wandering, this wing of the house had been cordoned off with two of Dasselaar's security personnel stationed at each end of the corridor, so I hadn't been able to explore any of the rooms off this hall. While the items that had been blocking this area of the house had been removed, the security presence was still strong. Two armed guards, their guns visible as bulges under their ill-fitting jackets, stood by the double doors to the room where Dasselaar had told us to meet and several others roamed the hall from end to end.

While we waited for our host to make an appearance, I matched faces to the profiles Felix had sent me and realized everyone in attendance was a high-powered shifter with an estimated personal net worth of at least five hundred million US dollars. Most had questionable ties to at least some level of criminal enterprise and a couple were flat-out criminals. None of the people assembled was an art thief or, as far as Felix had been able to discover, overly interested in *The Evolution of Man,* though each was an avid art collector in their own right. Inviting this group of people was a strategic move, and one I appreciated. As I'd suspected, Dasselaar was going to use this group to drive up the starting bids on all the pieces, which would in turn net him a fat sum of cash at the end of the night.

Dasselaar kept us all waiting in the hall, building our anticipation and testing our patience, until finally fifteen minutes after he'd told us to gather, he emerged from the room where the auction would take place. He clapped his hands and rubbed them together, grabbing our attention.

"Friends, thank you again for joining me this weekend. It is my pleasure to offer you an exclusive first look at the rare and very difficult to obtain"—he smiled slyly—"pieces. At the end of the preview, you will each be able to cast one private bid for each piece with Mr. Emil Mondvogel. Tomorrow evening, you will be able to actively bid on the pieces during the gala. Now, with no further ado, please follow me."

The security guards on either side of the double doors pulled them open and we followed Dasselaar into the room. A freestanding temporary wall had been erected not far inside the room to create a traffic pattern, and Dasselaar led us around the right side of the wall. The space beyond had been transformed from a medium-sized ballroom into a museum-worthy gallery. At a quick count, fifty artworks were on display around the room, each appropriately lit to best showcase the piece. I recognized several of the pieces as stolen on sight, but some were harder to place, either because they'd been stolen a long time ago or because their history was unclear. On the back of the temporary wall was a covered piece, and I knew what was underneath. If I had to guess, Dasselaar would show *The Evolution of Man* off last, in the hope that it would be the piece everyone wanted to bid on.

Dasselaar approached the first piece, then looked around the room, his brow creasing when he appeared to not find what he was looking for. He beckoned one of his security guards over and whispered something into his ear. The guard nodded and disappeared, returning a moment later with Dimitri's bicep clutched in his meaty fist. Dimitri didn't struggle in his hold, but I could see the pain on his face. My hands clenched into fists as I committed the guard's features to memory. He would pay for manhandling Dimitri like that. Dasselaar stood in front of Dimitri with his back to us. I couldn't make out what he said to Dimitri, but when he walked away there was a heartbreaking mix of impotent rage and resignation in Dimitri's bright green eyes.

I wished he'd look for me so I could reassure him that everything was okay, but while Dasselaar spoke about the first piece, Dimitri kept his eyes on the ground.

"My colleague"—he gestured to Dimitri, and I scoffed under my breath. Colleague my ass. Dimitri was his prisoner—"has a unique talent. Besides the adequate provenance documents I will provide with each piece, I have a way to illustrate the authenticity of each of these artworks. Mr. Crysanthos's skin can detect anomalies in paint formulations. If the paint used is authentic for the time of the piece and not an amalgamation of contemporary mediums designed to mimic the effect of older methods, his skin will blend seamlessly into the background colors so you will not be able to discern where his skin ends and the painting begins. If the painting is not authentic, his skin will struggle to settle on a color, instead trying to work through the individual shades used to replicate the color and contributing a muddy overall appearance of the colors."

Small murmurs of surprise and some of skepticism slithered through the crowd. Several people leaned in closer to the painting, excited to see Dimitri's talent.

"Mr. Crysanthos, if you please." Dasselaar swept his hand toward the painting, inviting Dimitri to step up to it. He hesitated for a second, and I watched Dasselaar, his jaw tightening until Dimitri finally held out his hand, his skin changing almost immediately to perfectly match the art behind it.

Gasps sounded around me, and several people nodded in appreciation.

"As you can see, this piece is authentic." Dasselaar turned and picked up the Vermeer he'd shown me at his gallery. "This piece, however, is not." Without being told, Dimitri approached the painting Dasselaar held and hovered his hand in front of it. Colors began to swirl on his skin, but the hue was muddy and, like at the gallery, the edges of his hand were clearly visible.

This time the murmurs of surprise came from all sides. Dasselaar's guests were clearly invested in the theatrics of this display.

Dasselaar set the forged Vermeer aside, and we moved to the next piece. This time, when Dimitri was called forward, his eyes found mine in the crowd. I gave him a reassuring smile, and the corner of his lips tipped up in silent acknowledgment.

For the next hour, we continued around the room in the same way. Dasselaar would talk briefly about the piece,

Dimitri would authenticate it for the crowd, and we would exchange small smiles and covert glances.

The collection Dasselaar had amassed was significant and exciting. If any of these pieces had crossed through my gallery, the twenty-five million I'd gotten for Niels Zwart's Lichtenstein would have looked like pocket change.

Finally, Dasselaar stood in front of the covered piece in pride of place at the front of the room.

"I have saved the very best piece in this collection for last. This is one of the most elusive pieces of art in human history, and I have done what many before me have tried and failed to do. I have procured the original painting, which has not been seen in decades." Dasselaar's smug and satisfied smile confirmed another of my hypotheses. He had invited Juno to the gallery just to rub it in that he'd gotten his hands on something she couldn't, which meant there were definitely going to be other thieves at the gala, and we were going to need to be careful. Very, very careful.

I'd drifted back to the rear of the crowd, watching as everyone leaned forward when Dasselaar's fingers wrapped around the yellow cord holding up the piece of burgundy velvet covering the painting. Dimitri's eyes met mine, and I smiled as the curtain fell.

And then the bottom dropped out of my stomach.

Dasselaar was mistaken.

He didn't have the original.

The painting he had was my forgery.

CHAPTER THIRTEEN

DIMITRI

THE SECOND I watched Quin's smile slip from his face, I knew something was wrong. A spike of anxiety settled in my stomach, and my suspicions from the first time I'd seen this painting at the gallery came rushing back. My skin had never behaved the way it did with this painting, and I didn't know what to make of it. In my gut, I knew the painting wasn't the real one, but I didn't understand why my skin was reacting to the painting like it was authentic. The only difference was the slight flicker of iridescence before the colors came through on my skin like the painting was real.

"Dimitri!" Dasselaar hissed, grabbing my attention. When I looked away from Quin, Dasselaar was scowling, the muscle in his jaw tight. He pointed at the painting, and I stepped forward, hiding my hand and the canvas from view. The antitransmutative drugs made my animal form inaccessible, but I was able to tap into just enough of that side of myself to shift a small portion of my skin. After an hour spent showing off for Dasselaar's guests, I was starting to get tired, and it took a lot more effort to make my skin respond. I closed my eyes and concentrated hard, and my skin warmed in a way that was becoming familiar. I opened my eyes and watched until the flicker that whited out all the color on my skin subsided, and then I turned, keeping my hand over the painting, so everyone could see the colors were perfect.

Almost.

To the untrained eye, the colors were exact.

But when I looked closer I could see the slightest variation in hue and could make out the edges of my hand where it didn't completely blend into the colors on the canvas behind it.

Looking at this now, I knew this painting was a fake. An exceptional forgery, but a forgery all the same.

And now, what had been suspicions at the gallery when I'd first seen the painting had become facts.

Which meant I had lied to Stefan Dasselaar.

A collective gasp echoed through the room as everyone made sense of what they were seeing, then everyone began talking at once.

Everyone except Quin.

The din grew deafening as Dasselaar's guests began asking him questions and talking excitedly to each other, but Quin didn't move within the chaos.

He stood stock-still at the back of the crowd, his dark eyes wide as he looked at where my hand hovered over the painting. Eventually, his eyes found mine, the dark depths filled with confusion. Quin knew something about this painting.

Dasselaar and the crowd moved toward the door where Dasselaar's banker, an owlish man I'd met only once before, was waiting to take their bids for the auction. Quin moved with them, and I tried to linger, hoping to fall into step beside him, but as soon as I began to move, strong hands grabbed my biceps from either side and held me still.

"Where do you think you're going?" Scar's voice made the hairs on the back of my neck stand on end, especially since I'd overheard him talking to Dasselaar the previous night.

I didn't respond, and his grip on my arms tightened. Instead of leading me to the door everyone else had gone through, Scar and the bear shifter on my other side tugged me farther into the ballroom gallery and through a concealed door that led into the unused service corridor.

A scream built in my chest, panic rising, as I imagined what Scar had planned for me, but he just led me down the stone halls until we came to a set of stairs. He shoved me up them, the other guard leading the way, and I realized there was something familiar about being in this part of the house. We reached the third floor near the linen closet. Exactly where Quin and I had emerged last night, and Scar pushed me down the hall until we were standing in front of my door.

"Mr. Dasselaar is disappointed with your performance today, so you will not be joining him and his guests for dinner. He said he will consider having something sent up, but I wouldn't count on it." Scar's lip curled in a sneer as he shoved me into my room and locked the door.

I wasn't wholly sure how I had disappointed Dasselaar, but I didn't really care. I wanted to know what Quin knew about that painting. Was that the one his brothers were planning to steal? Would they still bother if they knew it was fake?

If Quin's brothers didn't come here to steal the painting, would Quin still keep his promise to get me out of here?

CHAPTER FOURTEEN

QUIN

"NERO, the painting Dasselaar has is a fake. It's my forgery."

"You've seen it?"

"Yes."

"And you're sure it's yours?"

I rolled my eyes even though my brother couldn't see me. "Yes. I wouldn't have called you with this if I wasn't positive."

"Okay, but this changes nothing."

I pinched the bridge of my nose and sat down in the wingback chair in my room. I'd done the bare minimum in terms of socializing after dinner, finishing one drink before heading back up to my room. The guests on either side of me were still down in the salon or engaged elsewhere around the estate, but I wasn't naive enough to assume I had any privacy, so I kept my voice low as I filled my brother in. "Are you sure? Now that we know it's not the real painting, is it worth trying to grab it?"

"Cal, Jack, and I have been talking a lot about that. We

think whoever came after Felix is still after the painting, which means they will probably go after Dasselaar. Or his buyer."

"Right. So why do we need to stay involved?"

"Because once whoever the big bad is figures out Dasselaar's painting is a fake, this whole thing starts all over. We can't back down until we know who targeted Felix and we remove them from the game."

"And what does stealing the fake accomplish exactly?"

"It gives us a way to draw out the real threat."

"And I can't just paint you another one?" I wasn't serious, and my brother knew it, but this was all starting to feel a little dangerous, and I worried about people I cared about getting caught in the crossfire. I wasn't sure how Dimitri had managed it, but he'd somehow lied about the painting being real, and if Dasselaar—or his buyer—found out, I didn't want to think about what would happen to my mate. Maybe Nero was right and stealing the painting was the right move. At least we already knew it was a forgery.

Nero laughed. "No, but thanks for asking."

"So what's the plan? From what I can tell, the paintings are hung on safety hooks fitted with closed-circuit, independent pressure sensors. There is no way to get the painting off the wall or out of the frame without triggering the sensors. A smash-and-grab won't work, and Felix can't hack the sensors since they are off the grid." I'd been able to see behind *The Evolution of Man* while I'd been stuck in the bottleneck getting out the door to make a bid. By the time I'd gotten the chance, Mr. Mondvogel told me the highest bid was up to one hundred million dollars. I'd texted Jules, who'd almost cried but said he'd make the funds available in the account, so I'd bid one hundred and one million dollars and tried to affect nonchalance as I joined the others on the veranda for lunch, wondering the whole time who Jules was stealing the money from to fund this enterprise. Reuben's pockets were deep but not that deep.

"You let me worry about this part, okay? You just worry about getting your man to the pick-up spot for Hadrian."

Nero and company had decided the best way to get Dimitri out was to sneak him out in plain sight. With two hundred fifty guests, plus security personnel and plus-ones, there would be plenty of people around to distract Dasselaar. As long as he didn't keep a bodyguard on Dimitri all night, it should be simple.

But I wasn't holding my breath.

We were assuming Dasselaar would want Dimitri at the gala to use his talent to reassure the guests that the paintings were all real, but there was a chance Dasselaar wouldn't risk letting Dimitri attend. He had kept Dimitri locked in his room since right after the preview. I hadn't even seen how Dasselaar's goons had gotten him out of the gallery.

Maybe it was a good thing Cal had given me a gun after all. If I had to shoot my way out with my mate, I would. I just really hoped it didn't come to that.

Instead of telling Nero my concerns, I changed the subject. "Has Felix been able to do anything with the footage of the estate I took today?"

Nero's voice was full of pride when he responded. "He has a full 3D rendering of the estate done. He was able to take the plans we have and overlay the layout from your video so we can digitally plan a route."

"Good."

"What's wrong?"

"Nothing. Why?"

Nero sighed. "You're a terrible liar. And I have Cal over here confirming you're full of shit. He says he can feel it through your freaky twin bond."

"Tell Caligula he's a traitor."

Nero did as I asked, and a scuffle broke out on their end.

"You take that back, Quintillus!" Cal said.

"I won't."

"Fine, I'll forgive you if you tell me what's got you all twisted up."

I could feel Cal's concern through our twin bond, and I knew there was no escaping this. So I reluctantly gave in. "Dimitri somehow lied to Dasselaar."

"About?"

"About the painting being real. I've seen what happens when he tests a forgery with his talent, but this wasn't that. The colors were perfect, but I could see in his eyes that he knew it was a fake."

Cal chuckled. "Aren't you always telling us that you're the best at what you do? Could your forgery be that good that even Dimitri can't tell?"

"I don't think so. I mean, I am that good, but there was something that made him question it."

"So ask him about it."

"I'm going to, but what if Dasselaar figures it out before we get Dimitri away from the estate? He's going to kill him, Cal. We heard him talking about it last night. What if he figures it out and pushes that timeline up?"

"This is why we give you shit about doing fieldwork.

It's not that you're not capable, it's that you get too in your head. Contingency planning is one thing, but spiraling into what-ifs is another. Trust us, and trust yourself. You're going to get your mate out, and you're going to live happily ever after, and we're going to do everything we can to make that happen."

I wanted to believe my twin, but I also felt like I was in the dark. Nero wasn't telling me his plans, and I didn't know if that was because he hadn't figured it all out yet or if he just wasn't sharing them with me. And Dimitri added another complicated layer. It felt like everything was unraveling and time was running out.

"I know you don't believe me, and that's okay. But we've got this, Quinny. Now go see your man. We have work to do here. I'll make sure Felix works his magic with the cameras so no one sees you."

"Fine. Please keep me posted." But Cal had already disconnected the call.

A minute later my phone buzzed with a text from Felix letting me know the cameras were looping. It was still early, and I poked my head into the hall. No one was around, so I grabbed my lockpick set and slipped out of the room, locking the door behind me, so if anyone happened to check they'd think I was asleep.

I needed to talk to Dimitri, and I didn't want to wait any longer.

When I picked his lock and snuck into his room just after midnight, he was sitting on his bed, fully clothed like he'd been waiting for me.

He sprang off the bed and launched himself into my arms. "God, took you long enough to get here."

I pressed a kiss to the top of his head, loving the way it felt to have him in my arms. "Sorry. I was trying to wait until everyone went to bed, but it seems like it's going to be another late night for a few of the guests." I pushed him back, still keeping him in my hold, and looked him over. "Are you okay? You weren't at lunch or dinner."

He rolled his eyes. "I'm fine. Dasselaar was disappointed in my less-than-enthusiastic performance at the preview. He wanted me to be all smiles, but I couldn't do it."

Something sour churned in my gut. I wasn't sure it was Dimitri's lack of smiles that had annoyed Dasselaar. We hadn't been super obvious but we also hadn't been all that discreet as we'd stared at each other during the preview. I knew for sure Dasselaar was suspicious of me, and my gut told me keeping Dimitri locked in his room was more about punishing me than him.

"I'm sorry."

He tipped his head to the side, an adorable crease forming between his brows. "For what?"

"I think Dasselaar has picked up on my interest in you. I didn't mean to put you in more danger."

Dimitri's answering scoff was as cute as the furrow between his brows. "You heard him talking to Scar last night. I've been in danger since the day I met Stefan Dasselaar."

"You said before that Dasselaar found out you'd left Cyprus illegally and he's holding that against you, but there's more to the story, isn't there?"

Dimitri closed his eyes and blew out a breath. "Isn't there always?" He leaned his head on my chest, and I let his warmth sink through my skin until I felt it all the way to my bones. Until his quiet question traded his warmth for ice. "How did you know the painting is fake?"

It was my turn to sigh. "That's a long story."

He lifted his head from my chest and took a step back, gesturing at his room. "I have nothing but time." He swept his arm toward the small sitting area with a couch and two chairs. "Let's sit."

I took the couch, expecting Dimitri to pick one of the chairs, but instead, he settled next to me and curled himself around my body, leaning into me and dropping his head on my shoulder. Closing my eyes, I savored the moment. My mate was tucked against me, and while there were mountains of obstacles to face in our not-too-distant future, for now, we were safe and we were together.

Dimitri took my hand in his and threaded our fingers together. The move was so familiar it felt like we'd done this a million times, even though we'd only had our first conversation a day ago. But this was what it was like when you found your fated mate. It felt right from the very beginning, like a piece of you that was missing snapped into place. As I gave Dimitri's fingers a squeeze, I wondered if he was feeling the same thing.

"You were just about to tell me how you knew that painting was a forgery." Dimitri nudged my shoulder with his.

"And like I said, it's a long story." I blew out a breath. "I told you before that my grandmother is Juno Hunter." Dimitri nodded against my shoulder. "She raised me and my brothers after our parents died. My father had been following in my grandmother's footsteps, carving out a name for himself in the world of stolen cultural artifacts. My mother was an archeologist. They'd met in college during a summer internship in Cairo." I waved a hand. "Sorry, you don't need to know all that. It's not really relevant to the story."

My mate lifted his head and looked deep into my eyes. "It might not be relevant to the story, Quin, but it's relative to you. I want to know everything about you."

It was on the tip of my tongue to tell him about our fated connection, but I didn't let the words fall. Instead, I continued with my story as Dimitri resettled his head on my shoulder. "At any rate, Juno raised us after my parents died, and to say it was an unconventional upbringing is putting it mildly. She took care of us, made sure we were fed and clothed and doing well in school, but she also taught us tricks of her trade. Nero was her protege now that our father was dead, and by the time he was eighteen, he was pulling heists with her. Cal, my twin, was the wild one, so she'd harnessed his wildness with martial arts and weapons training until he joined the military, then went into private ops. Julius, the baby, was gifted with a computer and she pushed him to learn everything he could about coding. Jules ended up hacking a bank when he was like thirteen, and after that, his path to becoming a modern-day Robin Hood was pretty much set."

"What about you?"

"I was the artist." I held out my hands, and Dimitri traced the stains and calluses on my palms and fingers. "And I have almost an eidetic memory when it comes to art. She found me drawing *The Great Wave* from memory with a blue ballpoint pen when I was seven after a class field trip to the Seattle Asian Art Museum. After that, I learned everything she could teach me about forging art, and when her expertise ran out, she sent me to France and Italy for summers to learn from her friends." I turned Dimitri's hand over in mine, tracing my thumb along the veins there. "I recognized the painting as a forgery today because I'm the one who painted it."

"It seems we have something in common."

"What's that?"

"I'm a forger too. It's how I met Dasselaar. After my sister and I moved to Amsterdam, I tried to make a living selling my original art to tourists, but it barely made a dent in our bills, so I moved on to selling forgeries. I would paint pieces and take them to galleries, claiming they'd been left to me by a deceased relative. Since I can change some of my features at will, I would make my face just different enough that I couldn't be the same person. I became an expert at forging authenticity and provenance documents, and I used my talent to make sure the paintings were as perfect as possible. My sister is in art school, and she would sneak me into the studios after hours so I could study the famous pieces on display and use them to get my paint formulations exactly right. I only sold one painting at a time, and I spread them out so it wouldn't be obvious what I was doing. A little over a year ago, I tried to hustle Dasselaar. He figured out the painting I'd sold him was a fake and tracked me down. He told me the painting was one of the best forgeries he'd ever seen, and it had taken two appraisers to realize the painting wasn't authentic. He threatened my sister and locked me up here, forcing me to work for him in exchange for keeping my sister alive."

We were both quiet for a minute after that as I processed what he'd just revealed.

"Why did you lie and tell Dasselaar the painting was real?"

Dimitri shook his head. "I didn't. Something strange happens when I use my talent on the painting." He looked down at his hands, and I followed his gaze, my eyes picking up a faint glow around his fingers that reminded me of the way the inside of a seashell shines. "I've never had this happen before, but the first time I saw the painting there was this glow, then the colors resolved to be almost perfect. In fact, the first time I saw the painting, I couldn't detect a difference in hue at all. I didn't even notice the colors were off between my skin and the canvas until today."

"And that was enough to fool Dasselaar?"

"He was distracted when this glow started and only saw my hands after the colors had settled. That's why I stood with my body blocking everyone's view of the painting today."

Dimitri settled his hand on my leg, and the glow got brighter. He pulled his hand away, and the iridescent shimmer faded a little. When he held my hand, our bare skin brushing, the glow got the brightest, looking almost like oil on water, pinks, yellows, and greens catching the light.

With a gasp, Dimitri sat up quickly and dropped my hand.

CHAPTER FIFTEEN

DIMITRI

"OH MY GOD. I am such an idiot." I pushed off the little couch and started pacing.

After meeting Quin's brother, his twin brother, I started drawing him. Not the brother, at least not since the first couple of sketches, but Quin. I'd felt pulled toward someone I'd never met, but every time my pencil touched paper and the lines of his face appeared it felt like I knew him.

The iridescent glow around my hands started on the day I met him. I remembered now that Dasselaar had been distracted by the chime at the front of the gallery. It had to have been Quin walking in right as I started to reach out toward the painting.

His painting.

Until Quin's confession that he had forged the painting, I hadn't put two and two together, but now everything was crystallizing into a single thought.

Quin was my mate. My fated mate.

With all the antitransmutative drugs in my system, my

body couldn't react to Quin the way it was supposed to. Not that it would have anyway since Quin wasn't a chameleon shifter. But the iridescent glow was my body's way of reacting to him the only way it could, and maybe my body was protecting Quin somehow by reacting to the painting like it was real.

Either that or Quin was the best damn forger on the planet.

Maybe it was both.

Strong arms stopped me in my tracks and held me tight. My skin warmed at Quin's touch, and I knew my hands were glowing.

"What is it? What's wrong?"

I looked up to meet his eyes, and it was like something clicked into place.

"You're my fated mate."

"I know. I've known since the day I met you in the gallery. I think Cal knew even before then." He reached up and pushed the collar of his shirt aside to reveal the black skin on his neck. It looked exactly like I'd drawn it, the broad brushstroke vee. "All orca shifters have a saddle patch here." He slid a hand down my arm until his callused fingers wrapped around mine, then he lifted them to the skin on his neck, closing his eyes as my fingers connected with his skin. "It changes when we meet our fated mates. If you were an orca shifter, your saddle patch would look just like mine, a shared fingerprint binding us together."

My skin lit up, the glow that had circled my hand spreading up my arm and spilling onto Quin's skin. I knew if I could shift, my chameleon form would take on the color at Quin's neck, and I would know we were mates, but for now, the glow was all I would get.

Quin held my hand against his neck for a long time, his eyes still closed like he was savoring my touch, and I let myself enjoy the moment.

Until the reality of my situation came crashing down around me. Even if Quin could get me out of Dasselaar's estate and take me away with him, I couldn't go, not when it would put Athina's life at risk.

Quin squeezed my fingers and opened his eyes. "I'm going to get you out of here, and I'm going to spend the rest of my life with you."

It was like he had pulled the thought from my head, and I swallowed down the sob that threatened to rise from my throat. "It's not that simple."

"Like hell it's not. You're mine."

I shook my head. "It's not just me under Dasselaar's thumb."

"Then tell me who else, and I'll call my brothers and revise the plan."

"It's my sister."

Quin studied my face for a long time, then his eyebrows rose. "Athina?"

"Yes. She's my baby sister. She's the reason I tried to sell Dasselaar that painting. She's in art school here and she's sick. She has the same rare metabolic bone disease that killed my parents, only hers showed up when she was much, much younger. Without medication, her bones will lose density until she can no longer hold a paintbrush, walk, or eat. Dasselaar pays for her schooling, living expenses, and her medications."

"What was in the file you saw?" Quin cupped my face in his hand and tilted my head so I had to look at him.

"After he gets rid of me, he's going to cut her off. No more tuition. No more rented flat. No more medication." The sob I'd held back before escaped now. "She'll be dead within a year."

"No, she won't."

"She will. The disease progresses fast."

Quin shook his head, sympathy in his eyes. "No, she's not going to die because she's not going to have to go without her medications. We'll take care of it. Plus, there are some great art schools in Seattle, and my grandmother has lots of connections she can call on to get Athina enrolled wherever she wants to go."

I felt my mouth drop open in surprise. "You would do that?"

He pressed a kiss to my forehead. "It's not even a question. You are mine, and what is important to you is important to me. Your family is my family, and mine will be yours. Though please don't hold that against me, especially after you meet the real Cal who's not trying to be undercover on an op."

That little seed of hope Quin had accidentally planted finally took root, and something green and growing pushed its way up and into my heart. Maybe my prince had come to rescue me after all.

Before I could consider my actions, I threw myself into Quin's arms, my lips colliding with his. The kiss was sloppy and uncoordinated as I tried to put everything I was feeling into it, but Quin met my mouth with the same ferocity, like now that we had acknowledged who we were to each other he was done holding back.

His hands found my ass, and with a strength that surprised me, Quin lifted me up so my legs wound around his waist. We never broke the kiss, devouring each other's mouths like we were never going to get the chance to do this again.

And we might not.

Everything could fall apart at the gala tomorrow night—or anytime between now and then—and as quickly as Quin came into my life, he could be gone again.

We could be over before we even began.

Which meant I wasn't going to waste this opportunity.

Using Quin's shoulders for leverage, I pushed myself up, rubbing my erection against his and making him moan. I swallowed down the sound as Quin took several steps backward until his legs hit the edge of my bed and he collapsed onto it, dragging me down onto his lap. Quin's mouth left mine for the handful of seconds it took to pull my T-shirt off over my head, and then his lips were right back on me, our tongues tangling as his hands roamed over the now bare skin of my back and chest. His hands were rough, the calluses and strength in his fingers a contradiction to the perfect, polished, designer-clad shape of the man, and everywhere he touched left a trail of fire leading straight to my cock, which ached behind my zipper.

Sliding my hands out of Quin's hair, I moved them between us, my fingers fumbling with the buttons of his expertly tailored dress shirt. He hadn't changed out of what he'd worn to the preview, and despite being in the clothes all day, he still looked perfect, not a wrinkle anywhere, and the only hairs out of place were those I had dislodged as I tugged on the dark strands. Quin rested his forehead against mine, watching as my fingers worked over each button, and tugged the shirt from where it was still neatly tucked in.

"Yes." The single word was followed by a moan as my hands met the warm bronze skin of his chest and pushed the fabric of his shirt away. The second his shirt was gone, tossed somewhere behind me, Quin yanked me closer, melding our mouths and bringing our naked chests together. Shamelessly, I rutted against Quin's erection, needing more. No one would come looking for me until morning, so we had time, but I was desperate to feel Quin inside me, filling places that had been empty for too long.

Reaching for Quin's belt, I hoped he'd take the hint. One of his hands, which had been busy massaging my ass cheek, his fingers teasing my crease, traced over my thigh to where my hands were busy trying to undo his belt. He gripped my wrist, stilling my movements, and I pulled away from his mouth to look at him.

"I want you to touch my cock so badly, but I want to taste you first." His other hand moved from my ass to cup my dick through my pants, making me whimper. "Will you let me taste you?"

"Fuck. Yes, please."

Before the words finished leaving my lips, I was pulled tight to Quin's chest as he stood with me in his arms, then turned and threw me back onto the mattress so I bounced a little. His fingers were working open my pants and stripping me bare before I could catch my breath. When I was naked beneath him, he paused, staring down at me as he stood between my spread legs.

"You are the most gorgeous thing I've ever seen." His gaze slid over my body from the top of my head to my bent knees where they hung over the side of the bed. The reverence and awe in his eyes made tears threaten again. It had been far too long since someone had looked at me like I was precious, like I mattered, that I almost wanted to cover myself, to hide from his gaze even as it made me feel safe and wanted. After he finished taking me in with his eyes, he leaned forward, blanketing me with his half-dressed body, and kissed my temple, running his hands through my hair and using his grip to tug my head to the side so his lips could trail down my cheek, over my jaw, and down the column of my neck. Quin sucked at the skin where my shoulder met my neck, and my body arched off the bed as a moan fell from my lips.

Quin's hand slid up my chest, his mouth ghosting over my ear as he held a single finger to my lips and whispered, "Shh," against the shell of my ear.

"You said you were going to taste me." My words were breathy with arousal, and I almost didn't recognize my own voice.

"I am tasting you."

His mouth moved down my neck again, and he bit and sucked at my collarbone, his hands tracing teasing patterns along my abdomen. Quin was determined to go at his own pace, even if doing so drove me to the brink of madness, and I was helpless to do anything but enjoy his unwavering attention. His fingers found one of my nipples, and he rolled the pebbled flesh between his thumb and forefinger. A jolt of sensation raced down my spine, landing in my balls and making my cock leak. I could smell my arousal in the air, and I knew Quin could too. His mouth replaced his hand, and the warm heat of his tongue on the sensitive flesh made me cry out. No one had ever spent time worshipping my body like this, but it was like Quin knew exactly where to touch, and kiss, and bite, and lick to turn my entire being into a writhing mass of need and desire.

He turned his head, the rasp of his barely there stubble rough against my flesh, and gave my other nipple the same attention. By the time he was finished, I was panting and nearly desperate, but still, Quin didn't relent. He moved farther down my body, careful to avoid any contact with my dick, and his mouth followed every dip and curve of my abdomen. He kissed every freckle and swirled his tongue around my navel until I finally felt his breath against my cock. At some point, I'd closed my eyes, and I opened them as I leaned up on my elbows to look down my body to where Quin was staring at my cock, his strong hands holding my legs open wide.

"Perfect. Just so perfect."

Quin lifted his head, his eyes meeting mine as he lowered to his knees. He held my gaze as he licked up my cock from base to tip, his lips closing around the head, his tongue stroking across the slit. His eyes dropped closed as he moaned around me, savoring the taste, and my arm gave out, sending me sprawling back on the bed.

The attention Quin paid to my dick was just as thorough as the attention he'd given to the rest of my body. His movements were slow and unhurried, building my pleasure moment by moment instead of pushing me toward the edge at breakneck speed. Quin's hands caressed my inner thighs and rolled my balls over his palm until I was thrusting up into his mouth, begging for more.

"Quin, please. I need more. I need you."

My begging flipped some sort of switch in him, and the slow and seductive blowjob changed in an instant. Quin's head bobbed between my legs and he worked my shaft with his lips and tongue. Saliva slid from his mouth, dripping over my balls and sliding down my crease. The wet sounds of his mouth on my cock echoed through the room as he took me deep into his throat. I reached blindly for a pillow, smashing it over my face to muffle my cries of pleasure because I could no longer hold them back. Every fantasy I'd ever had of this man taking me apart paled in comparison to the real thing.

Quin's fingers slid between my cheeks, finding my hole and circling it with just enough pressure that I pushed my body toward his hand, looking for more. But Quin continued to tease, the tip of his finger barely penetrating my body as his tongue flicked against the spot on the underside of my cockhead that made my knees weak. He had positioned my legs over his shoulders, and as he finally pushed inside me a little farther, I began to shake.

"Quin!" His name fell from my lips on a needy whine as he wrapped a hand around my spit-slick cock and moved his lips lower, sucking each of my balls into his mouth, before continuing his quest. When his hot tongue lapped over my hole, I thought I would explode. "Oh my god!"

He pulled his mouth away, dropping a gentle kiss on my hole before I felt him smile. “I said I wanted to taste you.”

I could no longer form words, so I hooked my ankles around his neck and pulled him back down.

CHAPTER SIXTEEN

QUIN

THE SECOND I TASTED DIMITRI, I was addicted. I wanted to keep my mouth on him forever, but he was starting to get impatient.

"I've got you, beautiful." I whispered the words into his inner thigh and readjusted my grip on his body.

Dimitri whimpered as I pushed his firm, round ass cheeks even wider and tongued over his hole. This time, I didn't tease, pushing my tongue as far inside his body as I could, loosening him up with languid thrusts. His hips arched off the bed, and he squeezed the pillow harder over his face, muffling his sounds. I wanted to hear him scream his pleasure, and I wished we were somewhere he could be as loud as he wanted. For a moment before he'd grabbed that pillow, I'd forgotten we were at Stefan Dasselaar's estate, that Dimitri's life—and his sister's—hung in the balance, that my brothers were poised to steal a painting I'd forged. Everything had fallen away as my focus narrowed to only include Dimitri, who was on the brink of coming apart under my lips and tongue.

But I didn't want to tip him over the edge yet.

My body ached to be inside him, my cock so hard it almost hurt, but tonight was about Dimitri's pleasure.

I slowly slid my tongue from his body, dropping a sweet kiss on his wet hole as I fumbled for my wallet in the pocket of my pants. I didn't have a lot of random sex, but I was a firm believer in always being prepared, so I kept a packet of lube in my wallet. The tear of the foil caught Dimitri's attention and he pushed his pillow aside to look down at me. His hair was disheveled, the black strands sticking up in every direction; his cheeks were flushed, the dusky pink gorgeous on his olive skin; and his pupils were blown wide, black almost edging out all the bright green. He was the most exquisite thing I'd ever seen.

"What—" I held up the now open packet of lube, and a sexy smile spread across his face. "Yes. Please." He flopped back onto the bed and pulled the pillow across his face as I slicked up my fingers and slipped one inside him. His body clenched around me, but the muffled sounds coming from under the pillow were pure pleasure. I worked the single digit inside him as deep as I could until I found the spot I was looking for. When my finger slid over it, Dimitri's body went tight, his cry barely subdued by the pillow. I added a second finger, giving him a moment to adjust before I pushed in deep and spread my fingers to open him up. Dimitri hooked his ankles over my shoulders and met me thrust for thrust until he tossed the pillow away.

"Quin, I'm ready. Please. I want your cock."

In an effort to keep myself from rushing this, I'd left my pants on, a decision I now regretted as I was desperate to sink into him. But maybe it was for the best. I was so hard and so ready to feel the tight heat of Dimitri's body that I wasn't sure I'd make it more than two thrusts before I was coming.

Sliding my fingers from his body, I unhooked his ankles from around my neck and stood. He was absolutely stunning laid out on the bed, the pink flush from his cheeks spreading down his neck and across his chest. His cock was hard and leaking, precum glistening at the tip, and my mouth watered with the desire to lick it away again. Instead, I tipped the packet of lube so a couple drops fell onto the head.

"Stroke yourself while I get rid of my pants."

Dimitri immediately obeyed, his hands spreading the lube over his shaft, the tip peeking through the top of his fist.

I held the corner of the lube packet between my teeth as I kicked off my shoes and toed off my socks, then opened my belt and tugged it through the loops. In my haste to get naked and inside Dimitri, I almost ripped my pants, stumbling a little as I kicked them and my underwear away. Dimitri laughed, and the sound coiled around my heart, but his laughter died as I pulled the lube packet from between my teeth and slicked up my cock.

Positioning myself between his legs again, I lifted his knees so his feet were flat on the bed and pulled him forward. My slick fingers found his hole and stretched him one more time before I lined the head of my cock up with his entrance and nudged forward.

"Are you ready?"

Dimitri dropped his hand from his cock, nodded, and tried to push his hips into me to take me deeper, but I didn't make him wait, sliding inside him until I was buried balls deep.

When I was fully seated it felt like something locked into place, like this was where I was meant to be, and I paused, letting the sensation wash through my body and penetrate all the way to my soul. Dimitri was watching me with wide eyes, and I knew he was feeling the same thing. I couldn't wait to claim him so I could feel all his emotions like they were my own. With my eyes still locked with Dimitri's, I slowly pulled out and thrust back in. I kept my pace slow until Dimitri started to tremble, then I sped up, grabbing his hips and tunneling into his tight heat, until I felt my balls tighten.

"You're so tight. So beautiful. So perfect." Words of praise fell from my lips as I kept up a steady rhythm, making incoherent sounds of pleasure pour from Dimitri. Precum spilled from his slit, and I reached down to smear it around the head and stroke his shaft.

"I'm close, Quin. Fuck. So close."

I bent my knees, changing the angle a little, and a handful of thrusts later, Dimitri cried out, his body going rigid beneath me as his cock spilled over my hand and his body squeezed around me so hard my vision started to fade at the edges.

I drove into him, prolonging his orgasm until I couldn't hold back any longer. I cupped his face in one hand, his eyes fluttering open to look at me as I plunged in deep and came on a silent shout, our gazes locked.

Collapsing forward, I caught myself on my hands as my body blanketed Dimitri's and I buried my face in his neck, right over the spot where I would one day soon place a claiming bite, and breathed in his scent—wet earth, bright citrus, and something that reminded me of soft leather.

We stayed like that for long moments, both of us catching our breaths and coming down from the high of the moment. My lips were trailing over the tendons in Dimitri's neck when he spoke.

"Thank you."

I lifted my head to look at him. The question was clear in my eyes without me having to say anything.

"For tonight and for agreeing to help me and my sister."

Smoothing his hair back from his face, I stared down at him. "Tonight was the beginning of our forever. You are mine, Dimitri, and I will do whatever it takes to keep you and the people you love safe."

"Thank you." Tears gathered along his lower lashes and his voice was little more than a whisper.

"You never have to thank me for protecting you. Never." A single tear escaped, and I brushed it away with my thumb before I pressed a kiss to the spot and pushed up from the bed. "Let's go clean up. I want to hold you for a while before I have to sneak back to my room."

Dimitri took the hand I offered him, and we closed ourselves in the en suite bathroom. Fifteen minutes later, we were back in Dimitri's bed, his head resting on my chest, his fingers drawing intricate invisible patterns on my skin.

"Can I show you something?" Dimitri lifted his head but kept his chin resting on my pec.

"Of course."

He smiled wide, then draped himself over me so he

could reach the bedside table. The drawer slid open, and Dimitri came up with a sketchbook.

"What is that?"

Dimitri let out a heavy sigh. "The only luxury Dasselaar allows me to have."

The sketchbook was a luxury? For some reason that made me hate Dasselaar just that little bit more.

"When we get home to Seattle, I promise to buy you as many sketchbooks as your heart desires. Hell, I'll buy you your very own studio and outfit it with whatever you want."

Dimitri shook his head. "I don't need a studio."

"I didn't say you did, but if that's what you *want*, it would be my pleasure to give it to you."

He dropped a kiss on my lips. "You're going to be ridiculous, aren't you?"

"If you mean that in the context of, am I going to spoil you to make up for every second you've spent in this hellscape with Dasselaar, then yes, I am absolutely going to be ridiculous."

I got another kiss for that, and this time it turned heated, Dimitri nearly straddling my lap before he remembered he had a different goal in mind.

"Stop distracting me."

"Me?" I put a hand on my chest. "I believe you were the one who kissed me."

"Only because you're so damn perfect."

I scoffed. "Because I want to give you everything you've been kept from over the last year? That's not me being perfect. That's me being a decent human." My hand fisted where it rested on the duvet.

Dimitri noticed the reaction and grabbed my wrist, smoothing out my fingers. "By this time tomorrow it will almost all be over. A bad dream I can leave in the past." But there was something in his voice and in the way he refused to meet my eyes that made me think he didn't fully believe that. I had to believe it. At this point, my blind belief that everything was going to work out tomorrow, that we'd get the painting and Dimitri out of Amsterdam, was the only thing keeping me going.

"Exactly." I tried to put as much confidence as I could into the single word. "Now, what did you want to show me?"

Dimitri flipped open the cover of the sketchbook, and my eyes caught on a bridge I recognized. It was near Dasselaar's gallery, which must have been how Dimitri had seen it. He flipped the pages too fast for me to comment on it, and the other drawings sped by too quickly for me to catch more than a fleeting glance, just enough to tell Dimitri was immensely talented with a set of simple drawing pencils. I wondered what he could do with a studio full of art supplies so he could work in whatever medium his heart desired.

The pages stilled, and Dimitri ran his hand over the spread, smoothing the pages down. My brother looked up at me. His hair was styled and he was wearing a turtleneck, something I'd never seen him in before, but it was undeniably Cal down to the scar through his left eyebrow.

"When I met your brother, something about him called to me." Dimitri turned the page, and more pictures of Cal stared back at me. Dimitri kept turning the pages, and I noticed that Cal's features started to change. His scar and facial hair disappeared. His hair changed. Until the images on Dimitri's pages were no longer my twin, but an image I recognized from my reflection in the mirror.

"You drew me?"

"Before I even met you."

"How?"

Dimitri shrugged a bare shoulder, and I pressed my lips to the joint, wrapping my arms around him and pulling him closer. He leaned into my touch, making sure as much of my skin touched his. "I don't know. I knew the first time I drew Cal that something was off. Eventually, I started to draw him with different features until it was you filling the pages of my sketchbook. I thought I was being silly, but then you showed up in Dasselaar's gallery. I thought I'd somehow drawn you into existence, but then I realized whoever Cal was, you had to be connected to one another."

He handed me the sketchbook, and I thumbed through the pages, studying each picture. Dimitri tried to grab it back when the pictures went from innocent portraits to more erotic images of me in various states of undress. The most recent sketch was me naked and lying under a thin white sheet. My eyes were closed, but there was a look of satisfaction on my face. My arm was stretched out like someone had been wrapped up in it. The drawing was incredibly detailed. I could almost feel the crispness of the sheet in the lines Dimitri had etched onto the page.

"This is gorgeous."

"You are."

I shook my head. "You are incredibly talented, Dimitri. It has nothing to do with me."

He didn't say anything and kept his eyes focused on the page, his fingers tracing along the lines of the drawing.

"Does the reality live up to your expectations?" The question was vain, but I needed to know I hadn't disappointed him.

His face swung to mine so fast we almost knocked heads. "The fantasy pales in comparison to the reality, Quin. Even in my best dreams I never felt this happy." I didn't doubt his words, but there was still sadness in his eyes, and I was going to do everything I could to drive it out.

Dimitri turned back to the sketch, and I held him close, kissing over his skin and breathing him in until his head fell back against my shoulder and his breathing evened out in sleep. I carefully closed his sketchbook and tucked it away in the drawer, then lowered us so I could hold him in my arms while he slept. I wouldn't be able to wake up next to him, but I would one day, and after that, I would wake up with him every day for the rest of our lives. For now, the stolen hours were enough.

Too soon, the night faded into the wee hours of the morning, and though it killed me to do it, I slowly slid from Dimitri's bed and got dressed. He didn't stir, and with a final kiss to his forehead, I let myself out of his room and relocked the door, leaving my heart on the other side.

When I got back to my room, I had my phone in hand before the door was fully closed, and Cal picked up as I twisted the lock.

"There's been a change of plans."

Cal groaned. "Another one?"

"Another one. Dimitri has a sister. He won't leave

without her." I gave Cal the rundown of the situation, and we came up with an idea. When he'd dropped me off, Hadrian had scoped out a small service road that went to the back of the estate. I needed to get Dimitri out of the house and to the service road where Hadrian would be waiting. Once he was safe with our cousin, I would return to the party like nothing was out of the ordinary. When the auction was in full swing, I would slip out, rendezvous with Hadrian and Dimitri, and we would go to Dimitri's flat to pick up his sister, then meet everyone else, hopefully with the painting, at the private airstrip on the outskirts of town. We'd be on our way back to Seattle before the dust even settled.

The plan felt deceptively easy, and I couldn't let go of the unease that sat heavy in my gut. At this point, failure wasn't an option. I had made a promise to Dimitri, and I would move heaven and earth not to break it.

I prayed with everything I had that I wouldn't have to.

CHAPTER SEVENTEEN

DIMITRI

WHEN I WOKE up the next morning, Quin was gone. I knew he would be, but that didn't stop me from wishing it wasn't true. My body ached in the most delicious way, and I loved that I remembered exactly what Quin and I had done last night every time I moved or sat down. Having him inside me had been transcendent and so far beyond anything I had imagined. Being with him filled my heart with a joy so immense I thought it might explode.

I was riding such a high that I was largely unbothered by the fact Dasselaar kept me locked up in my room the whole day. Breakfast had been delivered with my morning dose of antitransmutative drugs, but even that didn't bring me down.

In a dark corner of my mind, I worried about whether or not I would actually get to escape Dasselaar's estate with my life, but if today was my last day alive, I refused to go down in a torrent of what-ifs. Instead, I focused on how I'd felt in Quin's arms the night before, on how safe and secure he made me feel, how cherished and loved, and I let those feelings fill me up until the shadow of what was to come hung far in the background.

At lunch, another tray was delivered along with my tuxedo for the evening. Unfortunately, it was Scar who darkened my doorway this time. The bear shifter wore an all-black suit and his usual predatory expression as he pushed into my room without knocking.

"Mr. Dasselaar told me to remind you that your role tonight is to make his guests feel confident in their bids. You will remain in the auction room, and I will be responsible for watching you." His leer made a chill race down my spine. "You will eat in your room before the event, and I will come to get you when it's time. Be ready." The *or else* was heavily implied, and he turned on his heel without waiting for a reply. At the door, he spoke over his shoulder, an evil gleam in his eye. "You'll also be getting a second shot of drugs this evening so there's no chance you can slip away in the crowd."

"What?" My stomach pitched, and I thought I might vomit. Did Dasselaar know about Quin's plan to get me out of the estate tonight?

Scar chuckled, the sound menacing as it bounced off all the hard surfaces in the room. "He wants the extra insurance. I think we have plenty of insurance already, but he's the boss." Scar shrugged like there was nothing he could do, then left, closing the door and locking it with a deafening click.

I had no idea what Scar had meant by insurance, but the what-if shadow I'd shoved away sprang up, pushing its way forward. If Dasselaar suspected Quin was up to something, everything could come crashing down. Quin could get hurt. I'd resigned myself to my fate. I didn't like it. I wanted the freedom Quin promised, but I'd made an odd sort of peace with the fact that I'd fucked around and now I was finding out. I knew how my story ended. But I didn't want that for Quin or my sister.

My stomach was in knots when dinner was brought to my room, and I couldn't manage a single bite. The walls of my room felt like they were closing in, and I was desperate to talk to Quin, but until I got out of my cage there was no way to contact him, and even then, I'd have to wait for him to find me. I threw on my tux, fingers shaking as I fastened the bow tie, and paced in front of my door, waiting for Scar to barge through. I was so lost in my thoughts that the sound of the key in the lock made me jump.

Scar frowned when he saw me standing at the door waiting for him. "You're going to need to take off the jacket and roll up your sleeve." I complied immediately, undoing the French cuff on the shirt and holding the black and silver cuff link between my teeth while I rolled up the sleeve. I wanted to fight, but it would be no use, so I just let it happen. It was nice to have something to bite down on as Scar shoved the needle into my arm. Cold trickled through my veins, and I swallowed hard against the metallic taste on the back of my tongue. When he was done and jerked the needle from my arm, he gestured for me to put myself back together.

"Dasselaar said if you don't behave tonight, I can do whatever I need to make you comply." He looked entirely too pleased about that as he led me from the room. I had every intention of doing exactly what Dasselaar asked of me, until Quin worked whatever magic he was planning to get me out.

Every chandelier and sconce in the house was lit, and guests were beginning to arrive, a line of black town cars and limos beginning to queue in the driveway as valets rushed out to greet them. Music and the scent of food wafted out from the large formal ballroom across the hall as Scar pushed me into the auction room. A few of Dasselaar's weekend guests, now dressed in formalwear, milled about the room. I wasn't sure what to do or where to stand, so I found a corner and tried to blend in, staying out of the way unless I was asked a direct question. I wasn't sure how I was supposed to make sure the guests were reassured about their bids, but I assumed Dasselaar would make me aware of what I was supposed to do in his own time. For now, I stood in the room like I was supposed to and watched as a steady stream of guests wandered into the space. Quin wasn't among them, and I tried not to be disappointed. I knew he had his own role to play in all this.

Finally, after an hour, Dasselaar barreled into the room with a group of guests. The women were dressed in designer gowns and draped in gold and diamond jewelry, while the men were in an assortment of tuxedos and military dress uniforms. He asked me to use my talent and everyone was appropriately impressed when he led them to *The Evolution of Man*. He brought through group after group, and I used my talent until I was almost exhausted. The extra dose of antitransmutative drugs meant it took even more energy to draw on the small part of chameleon form that made my skin react to changes in color. Dasselaar noticed I was starting to fade and directed everyone in the room back to the ballroom for champagne and hors d'oeuvres. Scar stayed by the door, and I slipped back into my corner, leaning against the wall.

Dasselaar had shut the doors, but I heard them creak open.

"This room is closed," Scar said to the visitor.

"I just need a moment. I find the large crowd to be overwhelming." I recognized Quin's voice and my heart leapt in my chest.

"Fine."

A second later, Quin came from around the partition wall. His eyes scanned the room until they landed on me, and he almost ran across the space until he had me wrapped up in his arms.

Scar had thankfully stayed by the door.

"You look incredible." Quin held my hands and looked me over from head to toe, then leaned in and pecked a quick kiss on my lips.

"You do too."

Quin smirked, and in the tux, he reminded me of a roguish gentleman spy. "This old thing?"

His joke made me smile, but it slid off my face when I remembered Scar's words from earlier.

"What's wrong?" Quin put a finger under my chin and made me look at him. "What happened?"

I shook my head and kept my voice low. "I think Dasselaar suspects something. He made Scar give me an extra dose of the drugs, and he said something about wanting insurance so I didn't slip away."

Quin cocked his head, and I could tell he was listening to Felix in his ear again. "Felix is looking into it. Not sure what he'll be able to find, but know we have several backup plans."

I was scared, and I didn't know what to say. Quin grabbed my hand, tugging me toward the partition wall where *The Evolution of Man* hung.

"Dance with me." He whispered the request against my ear, and a jolt of warmth replaced a little bit of the cold dread in my veins.

"What? There's no music."

"That doesn't matter."

I frantically looked around. "Someone could see us."

"That's why I brought you over here. They won't see us until they come all the way around the wall. We'll have time to step apart and pretend to be looking at the painting."

Quin pulled me into his arms, one of his hands wrapping around my waist and the other holding mine. I followed his lead, swaying gently to music only he could hear, and muscle by muscle, I began to relax until my head rested on his shoulder. I wished we could slip away now, but with the party still in full swing, my absence would not go unnoticed, so I contented myself with time spent in Quin's arms and a few stolen kisses.

The door creaked open and the sound of a crowd filtered in, Dasselaar saying something about his collection being unrivaled.

Quin and I broke apart, but he pulled me close enough to whisper in my ear one last time. "I made you a promise, Dimitri, and I'm going to keep it."

Then he was gone, exiting around the partition wall as Dasselaar's group entered from the other side.

CHAPTER EIGHTEEN

QUIN

IT NEARLY KILLED me to leave Dimitri standing in the auction room, but we all had our parts to play, and I was supposed to be schmoozing Dasselaar's guests in the ballroom, pretending the painting hanging in the gallery meant nothing to me.

The big bear shifter bodyguard with the heavy scar on his face gave me a menacing look as I slipped from the auction room. He touched his ear and said something I couldn't hear over the din in the hallway as the door closed behind me.

"I don't like that guy." Felix was back in my ear, the comm fully functional again.

"Me neither." I plucked a glass of champagne from a passing waiter's tray and waded back into the fray. The wealthiest from the upper echelons of shifter society were in attendance, and I recognized a number of faces from the profiles Felix and Julius had put together. A man I'd done business with before was tucked into a group of people across the room, and I was about to make my way that direction when a tug on my sleeve grabbed my attention.

"Mr. Hunter?" It was a female voice, and I turned to find an elegantly dressed older woman in a Valentino dress I recognized from this year's runway collection.

"That voice is familiar. Who is that?" Cal asked over the comms.

"Azzura Scivolo." Felix's response echoed in my ear.

"What is she doing there? Was she on the list?" Cal sounded confused.

Felix responded as I reached out a hand.

"Yes, I'm Quin Hunter. I'm afraid you have me at a disadvantage. You are?"

She took my hand in a confident shake. "Azzura Scivolo." She glanced over my shoulder, and her eyes narrowed. "Do you dance, Mr. Hunter?"

Something was up. I got the feeling she knew something I didn't, so I inclined my head. "I do, Ms. Scivolo. Would you care to join me?" I offered my arm and she took it and let me lead her out to the dance floor.

Once we were safely ensconced in the crowd, she leaned in close. "Where is your brother?"

"My brother?"

"Yes. Cal. I met him almost two weeks ago in Venice. He was looking for *The Evolution of Man*."

"He's not here tonight."

She smirked. "He's not here as in present in this room, but he is here."

"Ask her about her great-granddaughter," Cal said in my ear.

"How is your new great-granddaughter?"

The question made Scivolo light up. "She is well. Healthy and happy. Tell your brother I appreciate him asking."

I nodded, acknowledging the request. "Was there something you needed, Ms. Scivolo?"

She scanned the crowd again, then pushed me into a slow turn. "Be careful, Mr. Hunter. There are sharks in the water, and they smell blood."

"I don't understand."

"I used to know your grandmother well, and I know what *The Evolution of Man* meant to her career as an art thief. I met your brother in Venice and now here you are. I can only assume your other brothers are here as well, and if that is the case, then I know what you are planning to do."

"I'm here on my own merit, networking with potential new clients."

She raised a perfectly sculpted eyebrow. "You and I both know better than that." She turned us again, so I was looking at a vaguely familiar face I couldn't quite place. "I am merely providing a word of caution. There is more afoot than you think tonight. Be careful, and tell Cal and Jack to proceed with caution as well. If I know Juno, she trained you to rely on stealth and cunning, making you gentlemen thieves, but there are others who will not hesitate to engage at gunpoint."

Scivolo's warning made the hairs on the back of my neck stand up as the song drew to a close and I led her off the dance floor. "I will relay the message."

"And I will help you to keep up appearances. Come with me." With her hand still tucked into the bend of my elbow, she led me across the room to a wolf shifter. He was older, probably in his mid to late sixties, and had a rugged face with prominent features and thick gray hair. He was lean and rangy, the standard build for wolf shifters, and his dark eyes were sharp and assessing as we approached. He leaned down to kiss Scivolo on both cheeks before she directed his attention to me.

"Vlk Mazal, I would like to introduce you to Quin Hunter, one of Juno's grandsons."

The wolf shifter laughed, drawing the attention of several people gathered around us. "Another one? I should have known." His accent was thicker than Scivolo's gentle Italian lilt. "Certainly you are not still looking for the painting. It is just in the other room." The genial smile faded from his face a moment later, and his eyes narrowed. "Ah, I see. Now that the painting has been found, you plan to recover it."

Scivolo cut in. "Mr. Hunter here is just attempting to make some new contacts."

"Is that so?"

I nodded. "It is."

The wolf shifter gave me a sly smile. "Well, in this room, there are plenty of opportunities. That is part of the reason I am here myself. And to lay eyes on the painting."

"Eyes not hands?" Scivolo gave Mazal a skeptical look.

"Only my eyes. Just like you. Stealing it now would paint too big a target on my back. Besides, the problem with that piece has always been that once you acquire it, it is impossible to move. That is not something I am interested in. I've moved on to more lucrative pursuits."

"He's running guns." Cal filled in the blank through the comm.

"That's not half as bad as some of the people in that room." Felix's words were punctuated by the sound of his fingers flying across the keyboard. "Warlords, cartel members, weapons manufacturers, both legit and not so much. Mazal is just helping them move their merch."

I tuned out the conversation in my ear and refocused on Scivolo and Mazal.

"I understand we are in similar businesses, Mr. Mazal. I, too, specialize in moving certain things outside the normal logistics channels."

He scrutinized me from under his thick brows. "Then let me introduce you to some of the men I know. Maybe you can help them get into new markets."

Scivolo nodded, then patted my arm again and moved away from us.

"Did your grandmother send you?" Mazal asked when she walked away, then he shook his head. "No, don't tell me." He gestured toward a group of men standing in the open doorway leading out to a veranda. "I respect Juno, which is why I didn't kill your brother and his mate when they paid me a visit in Czechia, and it's why I will help you tonight. I have several men on standby outside. If you have need of them, they are at your service."

"I appreciate that, but like I told Ms. Scivolo, I'm just here to network."

Mazal nodded like he didn't believe me. "Fine. Then I shall help you with that too. Perhaps you and your brothers will remember this should I need your assistance in the future."

"We will."

Mazal nodded and held out his hand, sealing the deal

with a handshake. I hoped he never had cause to call in the favor.

He took me around the room, introducing me to a host of his acquaintances and colleagues as Felix ticked off their crimes in my ear. Mazal and I parted ways, and I stopped to look at the time and grab another glass of champagne to keep my hands busy and to look like I was simply enjoying the party.

I really wanted to go back to the auction room to find Dimitri, but while I'd been working my way around the room with Mazal, I hadn't spotted our host anywhere, which meant he was still entertaining his guests in the auction room. My mind was firmly on Dimitri and mentally running through the plan to get him out of the estate, so I didn't notice that someone had come to stand by me until he cleared his throat.

"Where is Juno?"

It wasn't the first time someone had asked about my grandmother that evening. Her reputation preceded her, and apparently her grandsons were one of the worst-kept secrets in the art world.

I was still trying to place the older gentleman's face. He seemed so familiar.

"I'm sorry?"

"Did she send you in her place?"

Something about this man raised my hackles. He was too direct, and there was something cold in his tone. "I don't know what you mean. I'm here as Mr. Dasselaar's guest."

"You mean to tell me that *The Evolution of Man* resurfaces after two decades, and Juno Hunter isn't interested enough to make the trip to Amsterdam to see it? She had us traipsing all over the globe hunting for that painting."

The stranger's identity snapped into focus then. Age had weathered Constantine Yang's face, but the panda shifter was still handsome. He'd been part of my grandmother's crew for a long time until he broke out on his own. It had been more than a decade and a half since I'd seen him at our house in Seattle before their last job.

"She's retired, Con."

The older man's eyes almost hit his hairline before his expression resettled. "So am I, but I'm still here."

"What can I say? Juno had a conflicting engagement."

Con scoffed, the sound almost cruel. "I find that hard to believe."

Before I could respond or make an excuse to extricate myself from the uncomfortable conversation, Dasselaar waltzed into the room and into the middle of the dance floor.

"Attention, everyone." He waited a beat until the room quieted. "Final bidding for the auction begins now. We will be closing the lots in fifteen minutes."

Con moved with the crowd toward the ballroom door, but I hung back, letting traffic flow around me like I was a rock in a river.

This was it.

It was time to save my mate.

CHAPTER NINETEEN

JULIUS

"THE MONEY IS STARTING TO MOVE."

Felix turned his chair so he could look over my shoulder. "Whoa. Dude, I thought I was bad. That's, like, a hundred different windows. How can you even watch all that at the same time?"

I shrugged. "It's my superpower. What can I say?" In truth, I'd learned the skill watching stock prices when I'd been a Wall Street day trader. I hadn't lasted long in the Big Apple. New York City made me feel claustrophobic. But I'd learned a hell of a lot in the two years I'd lived there.

Felix pivoted back to his computer. Like some sort of heist movie cliche, we were camped out in a black van parked along a quiet stretch of road behind Dasselaar's estate. We could see the house from our vantage point, but unless someone knew where to look for us, we were almost invisible, tucked in along the edge of a thick copse of trees.

"Quin, how are things looking inside?" Felix's voice echoed in the comm in my ear on a short delay.

"All good. Half the guests are in the auction room. The rest are in the ballroom and hallway."

After Quin had paid his half-million-dollar buy-in to bid on the artworks in Dasselaar's collection, he'd been given access to an encrypted app. Felix had been able to hack the app, learning that there would be no live auction element at Dasselaar's gala. Instead, all the bidding was done completely anonymously via the app. Only two people—Dasselaar and his Swiss banker Emil Mondvogel—had access to the administrative side of the app. Dasselaar decided when the lots were closed for bidding, then Mondvogel, using the account information he'd taken when he'd collected the buy-in, swept the money out of the buyer's account.

For someone who didn't even keep a copy of the guest list for the gala on his computer, I thought it was strange Dasselaar was putting so much faith in an app. Not that I was complaining because he was making my job a hell of a lot easier, but still, it was weird.

Another of the lots closed, and I watched the money move from the buyer's account into Dasselaar's.

And so it continued until only one lot remained open.

"This is it." I watched the lot close, then did a double take when the money was swept out of Gaspard Malveau's account. "What the hell does Malveau want with a shifter painting?"

Malveau was one of the only non-shifters in attendance at Dasselaar's gala. He was a Belgian jewelry and gold dealer known for his ruthless business dealings. According to the profile Felix had put together, Malveau's great-grandfather had built their family fortune on illegally and inhumanely mined conflict diamonds, and while there had been a push toward legitimacy during the intervening generations, Gaspard had seen the same lucrative opportunities as his great-grandfather and was now one of the most powerful players in the black-market diamond trade. I'd been able to ballpark his net worth at somewhere around five billion dollars. As far as we knew, he had exactly zero interest in the painting. According to everything Felix had been able to find, his fine art holdings were minimal and trended toward surrealism. If it had been a Dali, I might have been less surprised that he'd ended up the high bid, but neoclassical was not his thing. Which meant he was buying the painting for someone else, or he had a buyer lined up and he was using the auction to launder some of his own dirty money.

Felix turned around so fast I felt the breeze on the back of my neck. "Wait. Malveau is the buyer?"

"Looks like it. I just watched two hundred and fifty-seven million dollars leave his account."

Felix whistled. "Damn. He's gotta be planning to unload it to someone else for more than that. He's probably using it to launder some of his money."

I nodded. "You read my mind."

He shrugged. "Nah, these criminal types are just that predictable." Felix turned back to his computer. "Nero, the buyer is Gaspard Malveau. Are you in place?"

For a minute when we'd been planning this op, Nero had thought about not making a play for the painting at all since we knew it was Quin's fake, but Malveau buying the painting was a neon, flashing red flag, and I was glad he'd decided to move forward with the heist. My gut told me that even when we got the painting out of Amsterdam, this wasn't going to be over. Letting the fake fall into whoever Malveau was working with's hands would only prolong the inevitable. Someone was still going to be looking for the real thing, and if we had the fake painting, we could use it as leverage to draw out whoever that was and find out who had kidnapped Felix and put a target on our family. If Dasselaar's painting had been the real thing, it might have been different, but learning it was a fake meant whoever was looking for the real painting would eventually end up on our doorstep since Juno was still on the short list of people who had the skill set to acquire it.

While he'd agreed to go through with the heist, Nero didn't love the plan he, Cal, and Jack had come up with. Cal and Jack had done more recon and had found out Dasselaar had hired a small team of people to prepare the auctioned art for transportation, either by the buyer at the conclusion of the event or to be shipped through Dasselaar's gallery for an additional fee. The plan was that following the auction, the art would be prepped for transport while the guests enjoyed more of Dasselaar's hospitality. At the end of the evening, the winning bidders could take their prizes or they would be moved to Dasselaar's gallery for shipment. Nero had infiltrated the team and would have eyes on the painting. Cal and Jack were in another rented van, ready for Nero to give them the all clear to make the switch, the transportation case with the painting in it for a case holding an empty frame that hopefully closely matched the weight of the painting. Nero thought there were a lot of holes in the plan, contingencies he didn't feel like he could plan for in an environment he couldn't control, not to mention the number of people that would still be around the estate. Jack was banking on the number of people around being excellent cover, but Nero was less certain. After they had the painting secured, they were going to head into the heart of Amsterdam to get Dimitri's sister.

Before Nero could answer, movement on my screen caught my eye.

"Something's up. Someone just deposited the exact amount Malveau paid for the painting back into his account. Felix, are you seeing this?" Felix looked over my shoulder. "Ten seconds ago, this account was two hundred fifty-seven mill lighter."

"Pull up the transaction log. Let's make sure it's not a glitch on Mondvogel's end."

I did what he asked and tapped a finger against the screen over the transaction's initiating party. "AB Holdings Limited. I've seen that name before. It's a shell company."

Since Felix had been kidnapped by Agent Lance Cooper and I'd started following the money flowing into his accounts, it had been shell game after shell game, and I'd made next to no progress. Our cousin Marcus, who was a forensic accountant and the person who'd taught me everything there was to know about burying my financial trail, was working on unraveling the web back in Seattle, but that didn't help me now.

"Let me see if I can find anything." Felix's fingers flew over his keyboard. "Bingo! AB Holdings Limited has an approved flight plan for a private jet that's waiting on the tarmac at the same airstrip where Reuben's plane is parked."

Nero's voice came over our secure channel. "I like swapping the painting at the airstrip a hell of a lot better than going into the estate."

"Me too," Cal agreed.

"We've gotta get Quin and Dimitri out." I sent Marcus Malveau's transaction record as I reminded them of our secondary objective.

Nero grunted. "Agreed, but the sister complicates things."

Felix tapped at his computer. "I closed Quin's channel. What are you thinking?"

It was Jack who answered. "If we're going to swipe the painting at the airstrip, we won't have time to go get her. Felix, what are we looking at for a timetable?"

"It's tight. Flight manifest says the plane is on standby and will be cleared for takeoff at the pilot's confirmation."

"We have to make a choice. It's either Dimitri's sister or the painting. We can't be in two places at once."

I jumped into the conversation. "We don't have to be. Send Quin and Dimitri to get Dimitri's sister. She'll be more likely to go with her brother anyway."

"Do you think Quin can handle it?" Nero had always been oddly protective of Quin, even though he'd proven he could take care of himself.

I scoffed. "You treat him like he's fragile, but he has all the same skills we do, big brother. He learned to shoot right along with us, and if my memory serves he might be a better shot than you."

Nero growled. "He beat me at the range one time. One. Time. And that was more than a decade ago. He doesn't use those skills often."

Cal cut in. "Um, pardon me, but when was the last time you shot someone?"

"Irrelevant." Nero's response was mumbled.

Cal spoke over it. "Quin will be fine. We're not expecting trouble at the sister's place. He'll be in and out and meet us at the airstrip."

"And I'll be there. I'm armed too." Hadrian's reassurance tipped Nero over the edge.

"Fine," he begrudgingly agreed.

"I'm going to reopen his channel and we can tell him about the change of plans." Felix tapped his keyboard. "Quin?"

"I'm here. What's going on? I think I lost you for a minute."

"Change of plans. Grab Dimitri and get to Hade. You are going to have to go get Dimitri's sister, then meet us at the airstrip." Nero's instructions were clipped, but Quin confirmed he understood.

"Quinny, do you have that gun I gave you?" Cal asked.

"It's in my room."

"You need to go get it, then give Felix the all clear when you're back in place and can get to Dimitri." Despite Cal's earlier confidence that Quin could handle the extraction, there was worry in his tone.

With the auction over, a handful of people were beginning to trickle out of the estate, hustling to their town cars, expensive sports cars, and limos. Likely they were the sore losers of the bunch.

"People are already starting to leave. Hurry, Quin." We needed there to still be enough people inside to cause chaos when Felix cut the power.

"I'm already on my way back to my room."

"Good."

For a while, the comms went quiet, and I counted every heartbeat. No one else left the estate, and the security team that had been patrolling the perimeter stuck to their predictable routes. From where we were situated on the property, I could see the far side of the building where a row of vans waited for the auction cargo to be loaded, and an idea hit me. "Felix?"

He cocked his head my way, not looking away from the screen where he was watching Dasselaar's camera feeds. "Hmm?"

"Is there a camera on the east side of the building?"

Felix tapped a few keys. "Yep, got the feed right here. Why? What are you thinking?"

"Can you run the plates on the vans lined up back there?"

He laughed like I'd said something ridiculous. "Obviously. Give me a minute."

I went back to counting heartbeats.

"Shit, Jules. I've got AB Holdings Limited on one of the trucks. Looks like the company rented the vehicle two days ago in Utrecht."

"No way that's a coincidence."

Felix shook his head. "Definitely not."

"I'm in place. I've got eyes on Dimitri." Quin sounded ready, and I knew Nero's concern was for nothing.

"Took you long enough," I teased.

"Had to get my bag to Hadrian and make a quick stop."

I rolled my eyes. Of course Quin had grabbed his suitcase.

"All right. Cutting the power in three, two, one." The second Felix finished the countdown, Dasselaar's estate, which had been lit up bright enough that the building could probably be seen from space, went dark. Through Quin's comm, we heard the sounds of chaos erupting as Dasselaar's guests tried to get their bearings in the pitch-black maze inside the estate.

"Let's get out of here before we get stuck in traffic. We can run comms for the next part of this from the airstrip." Felix slid past me into the passenger seat of the van and set his laptop on his knees.

Nodding, I climbed into the driver's seat, pulling my cell phone from my pocket and tossing it to Felix. "Call Marcus. I want to make sure he got the copy of Malveau's bank records and tell him what we've got. Get him to start digging into AB Holdings."

Felix gave me a mock salute as I hit the main road, heading for the airstrip.

CHAPTER TWENTY

DIMITRI

ONE SECOND I was watching Dasselaar's guests mill around the auction room, some taking a final look at the prizes they'd just won while others gazed at the paintings longingly, disappointment rife in the air around them. A couple of people had started negotiating to buy the newly acquired pieces. Dasselaar was near the center of the room, surrounded by a gaggle of people who were all clamoring for his attention now that the business of the evening had concluded.

The next second, the room was plunged into total and complete darkness. For a moment, there was a pregnant silence, like people were waiting for the lights to flicker back on as though the blackout had been some kind of joke. But when almost a minute passed and the lights didn't flicker on again, all hell broke loose. People were pushing and shoving, and I got turned around, then knocked back into a wall, losing my bearings in the darkness as people swarmed toward the exit, hampered by the temporary partition wall where *The Evolution of Man* hung.

Even in the dark and in my confusion, I smirked, wondering if the painting would still be there when the lights came up. Would it be Quin's brothers who ended up with it, or would it be someone else?

A hand landed on my shoulder, and I almost screamed until I caught a whiff of sea salt and pine and heard Quin's voice at my ear.

"It's time to go."

I nodded, then realizing he couldn't see me, I spoke. "I'm ready."

"We're going through the concealed door in the wall." Quin's hand slid down my arm, my fingers tangling with his. My skin warmed at his touch as he tugged me along the wall against the tide of the fleeing crowd. Somewhere near the middle of the room, Dasselaar was bellowing for everyone to stay calm while also trying to give orders to his security team as people flicked on their phones, and small pinpricks of light danced around the space, the strobing effect making me a little dizzy. There was no way his guards were able to hear him over the panicked din that was echoing through the gallery.

Quin's hand ran along the wall, looking for the hidden panel. When he found it, he squeezed my fingers, then pushed me through. The hallway was quieter, but there were still a lot of people trying to figure out which way to go to get out of the house in the near darkness. We turned away from where the crowd was heaviest, slipping down dark corridor after dark corridor until we were at the back of the house.

"Do you know where you're going?" I hated to ask the

question, but since I'd never seen all of Dasselaar's estate I had no clue where we were on the property or in relation to the nearest exit, and I prayed Quin wasn't counting on me to guide us out.

"Yes. I took myself on a comprehensive tour of the estate yesterday, and Felix made me this 3D map."

I hadn't realized Quin was holding his phone, the screen lit up with the hollow image of a house, a white dot blinking to show where we were. A green dot seemed to indicate our target destination, and I was relieved to see we were close.

Noise at the other end of the hall caught my attention, but in the dark, I couldn't tell if they were coming our way or heading toward the ballroom.

"Felix, are we clear?"

Quin didn't respond but opened the next door and pulled me through, shutting the door with a quiet click.

"What's going on?"

"Felix said there were three of Dasselaar's men coming down the hall toward us." He whispered the words as he pressed me back to the space that would be behind the door. Cool tile met my hands, and I guessed we were in some sort of bathroom. I'd never liked the dark. I hated not being able to see what was around me, and in the dark I was almost completely blind, my chameleon eyes better suited to detecting the nuances of color than night vision. I wanted to ask Quin to turn on the flashlight on his phone, but I held the request back, too afraid that whoever was coming down the hall might see the light from under the door and give away our hiding spot.

Quin had me caged between his body and the wall, and as voices got closer on the other side of the door, my panic started to rise. If Dasselaar's men caught me, I would never get out of this estate alive. He was already not planning on letting me live, but I knew for sure he'd kill me if he found me trying to escape. If that happened, what would he do to Quin? I couldn't let anything happen to him. My heart was beating too fast, and I knew Quin could feel it hammering against his chest. He pressed himself farther into me, blanketing me in his salt, pine, and mint scent and running his lips over my jaw.

"I've got you, baby. You're okay. You're okay. Breathe for me." The words were whispered into my skin, and I closed my eyes, breathing him in and matching my breaths to his as I focused on the feel of his body against mine and the press of his lips on my skin. The panic started to recede, and the voices outside faded into the distance.

Quin held me there for a few more minutes, pushing away a fraction of an inch. "Felix says it's clear. Are you okay?"

I pushed off the tile wall, my knees a little shaky after the moment of panic. "I'm okay."

I felt Quin's gaze on me even in the darkness, and he felt for my hand again, intertwining our fingers. "Okay. Then let's get out of here." He slid his phone from his pocket again and lit up the screen. The glow barely made a dent in the darkness, but his hand in mine kept the panic from bubbling up again. He held the device out to me and pointed at the screen. "There is a door here, and Hadrian is waiting for us on the other side."

Silently, Quin moved to the door. He gave my fingers a firm squeeze, then dropped my hand. He needed both of his—one to hold his phone with the map on it and the other to open the door. The hinges let out a soft whine as Quin pulled the door open and peered into the hall. I couldn't see anything in the pitch black, and I wondered if orca shifters could see well in the dark. Then I realized Quin wasn't looking. He was listening.

"I don't hear anything. Let's go." His hand found mine again, and he towed me into the hallway, following his map down another hall and through another turn. There was no way I would ever be able to retrace my steps if I was ever asked to. The hall we were in opened up into a large room, and it felt somehow familiar.

"Where are we?"

"The kitchen. There is a service entrance through the pantry."

Another door squeaked on unused hinges and closed behind us. The space we were in felt small compared to the ample size of the kitchen, but we didn't stop moving. Quin pulled me along to the other side, dropping my hand again to feel along the wall. When another groan of hinges hit my ears, it was accompanied by the fresh scent of dewy grass and cool evening air, the faintest hint of something floral on the breeze.

The waning moon cast enough light that I could see a dark car waiting for us in the shadows of the house, and tears pricked the backs of my eyes. I was a few yards from freedom, and I could nearly taste it.

Quin grabbed me again, his hand landing on the small

of my back and propelling me toward the waiting vehicle at speed.

He stopped for a second, his head cocked to the side as he listened for something I couldn't hear, then he yanked the rear door open and shoved me inside. "Get down on the floor. No matter what happens, stay down." He slammed the door shut at the same time the man in the driver's seat flew out of the car, something metal in his hand glinting in the moonlight as he tucked it into his waistband.

For a second, I didn't know what was going on, then I heard voices. I pushed up enough to see part of what was happening through the passenger-side mirror.

Two large men emerged from the shadows. I couldn't see their faces, but I recognized their bulky builds. Bear shifters. Which meant the men were part of Dasselaar's security team.

"What are you doing out here?" The man who spoke had a low gravelly voice I didn't recognize.

"With the power outage and everyone trying to get out through the front, I had my driver pull around to the back." The lie fell easily from Quin's lips.

"There's no door over here." A spike of cold dread ripped through me. That was a voice I knew. The last time I'd seen Scar, he'd been standing by the auction room door, one eye on the crowd and one on me. If he was here now, that meant Dasselaar knew I was missing.

Quin crossed his arms, and I noticed a bulge under his jacket. "Well, I'm outside, and I'll be leaving."

He turned, but Scar spoke again. "Wait."

Quin looked over his shoulder, while the man who'd

gotten out of the car—I assumed it was his cousin Hadrian —kept his eyes fixed on Scar and his colleague.

"What is it?"

"Mr. Dasselaar has put the estate on lockdown. Something very important to him has gone missing."

Quin held up his hands. "I don't have anything."

"Then you won't mind if I search your vehicle. This missing asset is incredibly rare and valuable."

Bile rose in my throat at the way he said the words. He wasn't talking about artwork or a piece of antique silver. He was talking about me.

"Be my guest." Panic started to seep through me again, and I lost sight of Hadrian as he moved to the rear of the car and opened the trunk. "See? Nothing but my suitcase. Now can we leave?"

"Open it." Scar reached into the trunk while Hadrian and Quin shared a look.

I couldn't see what happened next in detail, but I saw Quin reach for the lid of the trunk, slamming it down hard. There was a fleshy thump and a grunt as the door rebounded and Quin slammed it down again and again while Hadrian fought with the second guard. He landed a punch to Hadrian's cheek, causing his head to snap back. The guard reached for his gun as the muffled thump of something heavy hitting the ground echoed through the quiet night. It was just enough of a split-second distraction for Hadrian to land a kick to the guard's hand, and his next punch landed on the guard's temple. He stumbled back, reaching for his gun again, and Hadrian kicked him square in the chest, sending him falling backward, his head knocking hard against the building, his face scraping along the aged brick as he slumped to the ground and stayed down.

"Get in," Hadrian yelled as he sprinted to the driver's side and wrenched open the door. I maneuvered myself into the space between the rear seat and the driver's seat as Quin threw himself into the car. Hadrian had the engine running before Quin closed the door, and we tore down the gravel service drive.

Quin was panting a little, and the scent of blood hung in the air, but he reached out to me, and I took his hand.

"Stay down until I tell you it's clear." Hadrian's eyes darted from the road to the rearview as we turned onto the main road leading from the estate.

Looking up from my position on the floor, I took Quin in, searching for any visible injuries. "I smell blood. Are you hurt?"

Quin shook his head. "No. I'm fine. Hadrian has a small cut on his cheek." Quin glanced at the front seat. "I guess introductions are in order. Dimitri, this is my cousin Hadrian. Hade, this is my mate, Dimitri."

Hadrian smiled wide in the rearview mirror. The glow from the dash and the cut still oozing dark blood on his cheek gave him a sinister look, but his voice was kind when he spoke. "It's nice to meet you, Dimitri. Welcome to the family."

"Thank you."

Hadrian's eyes darted from the road to the mirror again. "I think we're clear. No one is following us. You can get up."

My legs were starting to cramp, so I gratefully climbed onto the seat and tucked myself against Quin's side, soaking up his warmth and letting the feel of his heartbeat drive away the last of my fear.

"There's been a slight change of plans."

Besides getting the painting out of Dasselaar's estate, the only other plan was to get my sister. My heart pitched in my chest. Maybe Quin's brothers had decided taking her with us would be too much trouble. If that were the case, I would get to her myself and we would run. It would hurt like hell to leave Quin so soon after I found him, but I would kill tigers with my bare hands to keep Athina safe, even if it meant breaking my own heart.

Quin must have seen something in my eyes that worried him, and he reached out to check the locks on the door were engaged. "It's about your sister."

I knew it. I fucking knew it. He was going back on his word. "You promised you would take her too. If you're going back on that promise, I've gotta get to her." The words came out on a sob as I pushed away from Quin, shrugging off his touch that a second ago had been so comforting. "Hadrian, stop the car." He glanced at me in the mirror but didn't take his foot off the accelerator.

"Calm down, love." Quin's tone was placating. "We're still going to get her. Only, it's not my brothers doing the pick-up. The terms of the heist changed, so we have to be the ones to go get her."

I let his words penetrate, and I deflated. "Oh, thank god. I really didn't want to give you up."

Hadrian laughed from the front seat.

Quin's fingers wove between mine as I thought of what it was going to be like to see my sister without Dasselaar or one of his goons looming over us, monitoring every word of our conversations. Over the last year, I'd only gotten to see my sister a handful of times, and I hated it. I just wanted everything to feel normal again. I wanted to be in charge of my own life, and I was so close to that reality.

"What is Seattle like?"

Quin rested his head against the top of mine. "It's a really interesting mix of natural beauty and big city. The mountains and the water are beautiful, but the city is full of great coffee shops and amazing restaurants. There are tons of parks and festivals and things to explore. It's busy, but you can always find somewhere to relax. I love it."

"It sounds wonderful." And it really did.

"Weather-wise, it doesn't get super hot or super cold, and if it does, it's only temporary. We get a bad rap for being rainy and overcast, and while that's sometimes true, there are plenty of sunny days too."

I nodded because that sounded fine. I'd gotten used to the cooler weather and less sunny days living in Amsterdam. I would never love freezing weather, but I'd learned to tolerate it. I wasn't worried about the weather. After a year in captivity, I didn't know what I was supposed to do without someone dictating my every move. It was going to take some getting used to.

As if reading my mind, Quin gave my fingers a squeeze. "You can take your time settling in and getting used to things. You don't need to make any decisions right now."

But I kind of did.

"Where am I going to live?"

"With me. It's an orca thing, but we tend to live in big matrilineal family groups. My brothers and I share a house that has plenty of room for our mates and our families."

"What about Athina?"

"I said families. That means your sister too if she wants to stay at the house. If not, we can help her find a place to live."

It felt like Quin was prepared to give me an awful lot, and while we knew we were fated mates, we hadn't claimed each other yet. Maybe Quin was waiting until he figured out if he could stand living with me before he tied us together in a way that couldn't be undone.

Again, like he'd plucked the thought from my head, he leaned in close to my ear. "I can't wait to show you my studio when we get home. It's the one place that is one hundred percent mine." His teeth grazed over my ear, then down to my shoulder. He brushed featherlight kisses to the back of my neck until his lips hovered over the spot where he would place a claiming bite. "I'm going to lay you out and fill you up and claim you in the only place that has ever belonged solely to me."

He bit down gently, making my eyes roll back in my head. In my mind, I could see the sun-dappled studio, smell the oil paint and fresh canvas, and feel Quin's body as his hands caressed my skin and his cock slid into me. He wasn't waiting because he thought we weren't going to fit. He was waiting because he wanted the moment to be perfect and I couldn't argue with that.

I let myself relax in Quin's arms, dozing a little as I imagined the rest of our lives together and Hadrian navigated the dark streets of Amsterdam. I had never felt so safe and wanted before, and I reveled in the security of Quin's embrace.

When the car slowed and came to a stop, I opened my

eyes, and in the single blink of an eye, my bubble of contentment burst, my heart plummeting to my feet so fast I thought I was going to pass out.

The cheerful blue door that led to our flat above the little bookshop was ajar, the wood splintered and broken, shards littering the ground.

CHAPTER TWENTY-ONE

QUIN

MY HEART CRACKED and splintered like the door to Dimitri's apartment as he let out an inhuman sound of pain. He scrambled out of my embrace, reaching for the car door, but I wrapped him in my arms, pulling him into me, trying to keep him from running headlong into a situation we knew nothing about.

Dimitri struggled in my hold, scratching at my arms as tears fell down his face. "Let me go! I have to go in! Let me go, goddamn it!" But I just held him tighter.

"Whoever broke the door could still be inside. I'm not going to let you put yourself in danger."

"She's my sister!" His scream clawed at my insides as his nails clawed at the skin of my arm, but still, I didn't let him go. If the worst had happened, I didn't want Dimitri to be the one to find his sister's body. Dimitri continued to fight me, but I wouldn't release him. Not until we knew what had happened.

Hadrian looked at me over the front seat, and I nodded. "Go."

He was out of the car in an instant, his gun in his hand as he toed open the broken door and disappeared into the darkness beyond.

Moments later, his voice echoed in my ear through the comm device I was still wearing.

"The place is trashed, Quin. Signs of a struggle. No blood, but she's not here."

"Fuck." As a rule, I didn't swear, but given the situation, there was nothing else to say.

Dimitri stopped fighting to look at my face. "What? What is it?"

I cupped his face between my hands, my thumbs attempting to stem the steady stream of tears. "She's gone, baby. She's not here."

"This is my fault. It's all my fault."

He closed his eyes, but I didn't drop my hands. "This isn't your fault. How could it be?"

A shuddering sob tore from his chest. "It's Dasselaar. He has her." His eyes popped open. "The insurance. She was the insurance."

"What are you talking about?"

"When Scar came to give me the extra dose of antitransmutative drugs, he said he thought they had enough insurance. He meant Athina. I know he did."

Felix had closed our channel so we wouldn't hear what was happening during the heist at the airstrip, so I couldn't reach him through the comms. But I wasn't sure what to do next, so I pulled my phone from my pocket and dialed Julius. He picked up on the second ring.

"Quin? Is everything okay?"

"No. Athina is missing. The apartment is trashed, and she's not here."

"Fuck."

"My sentiments exactly." Dimitri had rested his head against my chest, all the fight evaporated out of him, but I felt the wetness of his still-falling tears soaking into my shirt as his body shook with quiet sobs. "I'm not sure what to do next." What I wanted to say was that I felt helpless, adrift, completely unsure of what to do to make my mate feel better.

"Let me give Nero a status update, and I'll call you right back."

"Okay."

Julius hung up without saying goodbye, the urgency evident. While Dimitri and I waited for him to call back, Hadrian emerged from the building and slid into the driver's seat again.

"I'm waiting for word on what to do next."

He nodded. "I heard. Good plan to call them."

My phone buzzed in my hand, and I tapped the screen to answer it. Julius started speaking immediately, not bothering with a greeting.

"Nero says to grab whatever you think she's going to want or need from the apartment and meet at the airstrip ASAP."

"Okay. We can do that."

"Good. See you soon." He hung up again, the phone going dead against my ear.

"What's the plan?" Hadrian asked from the front seat.

Dimitri lifted his head and wiped at his eyes and nose. He was a mess, his big green eyes red-rimmed and wrecked, his cheeks a mottled red, and his nose running, but he was still the most beautiful thing I'd ever seen, and I would move heaven and earth to take away his pain in any way I could.

"Nero said to grab anything she might need or want from the apartment and meet them at the airstrip."

Dimitri immediately grabbed for the door handle, pushing the door open and climbing out of the car almost before I'd finished speaking.

Hadrian and I were a heartbeat behind, but he was already halfway up the interior stairs before we caught up to him. He took a deep breath as he stood before the apartment door, his hand suspended in midair like he wasn't sure he wanted to reach out and turn the handle.

I grabbed his hand and held it tight in mine. "I'm right here. It's okay."

But it wasn't. I'd witnessed the pain Nero had endured when Felix had been taken, and I knew how horrible it would feel if my brothers were missing. I would burn the city to the ground if anyone tried to take Dimitri from me. And if I thought it was my fault...I couldn't imagine the guilt, nor could I take it away. All I could do was exactly what I was doing—standing next to Dimitri and offering every ounce of support I could.

Reaching out, I twisted the doorknob in my hand and pushed the door open.

The apartment beyond was a disaster. Chairs were overturned, an easel lay on its side, broken, half-finished canvases bent and cracked around it. Painting supplies were strewn all over the place, and the cushions from the couch were tossed, one ripped open, fluffy white guts spilling out onto the floor. Either whoever had come to take Dimitri's sister had staged the scene to make it look like there had been a struggle or Athina had put up one hell of a fight.

Dimitri walked to one of the canvases and gently picked it up, studying it before leaning the broken piece against the frame of the couch. He surveyed the rest of the living room, his fist pressed to his lips, but didn't touch anything else. There was nothing left to be saved.

With a gentle hand on his shoulder, I steered him out of the wreckage. "Where is Athina's bedroom? We should try to gather some of her clothes."

Dimitri nodded and led Hadrian and me down a short hallway. The door to Athina's bedroom was open, but the damage inside wasn't as bad. The duvet was off the bed, dragged until it had caught on the leg of a small, worn vanity table that had pulled away from its spot near the wall. Other than that, the room looked normal. All the drawers were intact and the armoire was closed.

"Does she have a bag or a suitcase?"

Dimitri glanced up at me like he'd forgotten I was there, and while I moved to the armoire to look for something to gather Athina's things into, Hadrian led him to the bed and made him sit down. A growl rumbled in my chest when Hadrian wrapped an arm around his shoulders and Dimitri leaned into him.

"Easy, Quin. I have a mate. I'm not moving in on your man." I unclenched my fists, and my cousin smiled. "It's wild isn't it?"

"What?" The single word came out through clenched teeth, and I whipped the armoire door open with more force than was strictly necessary, making the whole piece of furniture wobble.

"How the second you find your mate, your world becomes all about protecting them, keeping them safe, making them happy." My cousin's tone went wistful, and I knew he was thinking about his mate, Ben, who was back in Seattle with Marcus. "They become your whole world, the sun and all the stars."

I looked at Dimitri who was staring at the wall, held up by Hadrian's arm and nothing else, and nodded. "I would do anything to take this pain away from him. Anything."

A wicked smile spread across Hade's face. "You're going to get your chance."

Turning back to the armoire, I found a worn duffel bag and started pulling things off the hangers, stuffing everything I could into the duffel before moving to the drawers and emptying the contents into the bag too. When I was done, I knelt in front of Dimitri and grabbed his face between my hands. "I have as many of Athina's clothes as I could fit in this bag. Can you think of anything else she needs?"

It took a long time for Dimitri's eyes to focus on me, and I was worried he was in shock, that the events of the evening had been too much for him. He'd barely escaped Dasselaar only to find out his captor now had his sister. It was too much to process in too short a period of time, and his mind was protecting him the best way it could by shutting down. He blinked twice, and I saw a tiny spark reappear in his otherwise dead eyes.

"Her medicine. She needs her medicine."

"Okay. I'll get it. Where is it?" I rubbed my fingers over

Dimitri's cheeks which were pale under the red splotches left over from his tears.

"Kitchen. In the refrigerator."

"Let's grab it on the way out." Hadrian stood and helped Dimitri to his feet, holding him up on one side while I shouldered the duffel and wrapped my arm around him from the other side, pressing a kiss to his hair. "It's going to be all right, Dimitri. We are going to get your sister back."

The hallway was too narrow for us to walk three wide, so I passed the duffel to Hadrian, who walked ahead of us, going to the kitchen to retrieve Athina's medication. He tucked it into the bag and slung it back over his shoulder.

"Is there anything else?" Dimitri was starting to shake in my arms, but he stepped out of my hold and moved to the far end of the couch where it was pressed up alongside the window. He slid his hand into the small space between the window and the arm of the sofa and came up with a battered, leather-bound sketchbook.

He clutched the book to his chest and nodded. "That's everything."

Hadrian led the way out of the apartment, and I wrapped my arm around my mate again, keeping him steady as we descended the stairs. Hadrian tossed the duffel into the trunk and was just about to shut the door when I remembered something.

"Wait." I settled Dimitri on the plush leather back seat, then rounded the car and fumbled in my suitcase until I found what I was looking for.

I climbed into the car next to Dimitri, who was staring at the broken door to his old apartment, while Hadrian started the car.

"Here. I thought you might want this." I held my offering out to Dimitri, who slowly turned away from the scene outside his window.

His eyes went wide as he looked from what I was holding to me and then back. "How did you get this?"

"I snuck into your room during the gala. You said it brought you comfort, and I wanted you to have it with you."

"Thank you." The tiniest smile lifted the corners of his lips as he took his sketchbook from me and stacked it with his sister's, holding both against his chest like he was using the books to hold himself together.

"You're welcome." There was nothing more to say, so I set my hand on his leg, squeezing gently and trying to send as much of my warmth into him as I could as Hadrian sped toward the private airstrip.

"No. Hell no. I'm not getting on that plane without my sister."

Dimitri's fire had returned on the drive to the outskirts of Amsterdam. Nero, Cal, and Jack had managed to steal the painting from the cargo hold of the other private jet, and it was now safely secured in the cargo hold of Reuben's jet, ready to head back to Seattle. Hadrian was working his way through the preflight checks and the plane would be ready to wheels-up in less than twenty minutes.

My older brother crossed his arms and narrowed his eyes at my mate. "You need to get out of Amsterdam. The longer you stay here, the more likely it is that Dasselaar is going to track you down. You're safe now, but every minute you stand here arguing with me is another minute I can't guarantee you'll stay that way."

"I'm not leaving my sister behind." Dimitri mirrored Nero's posture, the sketchbooks still crushed between his chest and folded arms.

"Nero, we promised to get his sister out."

Nero rubbed the bridge of his nose. "And we will. I just need to get the painting and your mate out of here first. Then we'll come up with a plan."

Dimitri's jaw was set. "Not good enough."

Watching my mate go toe to toe with Nero was hot as hell, but he also had a point. We'd—I'd—made a promise, and I wasn't going back on it.

Jack poked his head through the open door of the plane. "What's the hold-up? You ready to go?"

Nero waved him away, which just made Jack curious. He walked down the stairs to join us on the tarmac with Cal close behind. Felix and Julius filled the doorway, watching the standoff.

"I'm not leaving without my sister," Dimitri repeated.

Cal cracked his knuckles. "Then let's go get her. I haven't gotten to shoot anyone yet."

Nero sighed and pinched the bridge of his nose again. "We need to get the painting out of Amsterdam, and it's best if Dimitri and Quin go too."

Cal raised his hand like he was waiting to be called on, and Nero rolled his eyes. "What?"

"We have two planes, remember?"

Jack smiled. "Yeah, that's right. Send Hadrian back to Seattle on this one. Add Dimitri and Quin to the flight manifest. If Dasselaar is looking for them, it will throw him off the scent. We can go back to the hotel and regroup, then go get Dimitri's sister."

"We don't know where she is."

"Yes, we do," Felix called from the doorway. "I pulled footage from the traffic cameras around her apartment and a set of cameras on Dasselaar's estate that we weren't watching. He's holding her there."

A shudder rolled through Dimitri, and I wrapped my arm around him and leaned in close, speaking so only he could hear me. "You don't have to go back there. You can get on the plane and get out of here. I'll stay to make sure Athina is safe."

He shook his head. "I need to see with my own eyes. I have to."

I nodded. "Okay." My attention returned to Nero. "We're not going without her. It's not negotiable. If you want to go, fine. Dimitri and I will get Athina from Dasselaar's estate on our own." I used my most professional tone and touched the gun that was tucked into my waistband at the small of my back. "I still have the gun Cal gave me."

"Would you leave my sister behind?" Felix asked.

"You don't have a sister," Nero growled, shaking his head. "Fine. Cal, tell Hade he's flying solo."

"I'll go back with him." Julius pushed Felix out of the way so he could see our brother. "I need to see if Marcus has been able to trace AB Holdings any further than I could."

"Okay. Tell Hade about the change in plans. The rest of us are going back to the hotel. Jack, call Reuben and let him know we're going to need a pilot. Cal, you're driving."

While Nero issued orders, Felix and Julius ducked back inside the plane. Felix emerged, hustling down the stairs with his laptop bag slung over his shoulder, a few seconds later, and the muscle in Nero's jaw ticked. "Where do you think you're going?"

Felix stood on his tiptoes and locked his lips with Nero's in a passionate kiss that made my brother uncross his arms so he could hold on to his mate. When Felix finally broke the kiss, he rested his forehead against Nero's. "Where you go, I go."

Nero's jaw worked again. "Fine. Let's get out of here before we draw any more unwanted attention." He grabbed Felix's hand and tugged him toward the surveillance van.

Using the arm I still had wrapped around Dimitri, I urged him to follow.

"Thank you." His words were a little watery, and I saw tears shimmering at the edges of his eyes again now that he wasn't fighting with my brother.

"For what?"

"Keeping your promise."

I squeezed him tighter and prayed we would actually be able to deliver.

CHAPTER TWENTY-TWO

DIMITRI

"I'M GOING WITH YOU."

Quin spun to face me, a stormy scowl on his face. "No, you aren't."

"Yes, I am. Athina is my sister."

My mate rubbed a hand over his face and blew out a breath, then he closed the distance between us and put his hands on my shoulders, leaning his head close. "Dimitri, I barely got you out of there once. I can't let you put yourself in danger by going back."

"This time we'll have backup." I looked around him at his scary-as-hell older brother, his twin, and his twin's mate. They were all stacked heavy with muscle, and in the few hours I'd spent with them, I'd learned Cal and Jack both had long kill lists from the military and as private contractors, and Nero had worked with their grandmother on some of the highest profile art heists in recent history.

And that was before I factored in Felix, who was bent over a laptop, hacking into all of Dasselaar's security feeds again and setting up new loops.

They were a skilled set of men, and I knew they could keep me safe.

Quin closed his eyes. "Dimitri, please."

I cupped his face in my hands, holding his head until he opened his eyes to look at me. "Quin, I have to do this. I have to."

He sighed again, this time the sound was one of resignation rather than frustration. "Fine, but promise me you'll do whatever they tell you to."

"I will. I swear. I just have to know she's okay."

"I know." He pressed a sweet kiss to my forehead, then lowered his hands from my shoulders and twined his fingers with mine before turning to face his brothers. "Dimitri is going and so am I. What do we have to do?"

For the next hour, we hashed out a plan. It was simple. Sneak into the estate the way Quin and I had escaped, split up into teams, search the estate, find Athina, and sneak out the way we'd come in.

Easy.

No problem.

As long as we didn't run into any of Dasselaar's goons, especially since I didn't think Scar would be too happy to see us after Quin had slammed his head in the trunk of the car.

"Okay, I think we're ready. Everybody get some sleep. We're going in at first light." Nero stood from where he'd been perched on the arm of an antique couch that didn't look like it could hold his weight while he'd looked over his mate's shoulder at the laptop screen. Felix followed him into their bedroom.

Cal and Jack slipped into their room as well, until it was

just me and Quin left in the living room. I could tell from the tense lines of his body that he wasn't happy about me going back to the estate, but I had no choice. He had to know that, and as his eyes connected with mine, I saw his understanding and his worry, and I loved him just a little more for it.

I held out my hand to him. "Come on. Let's go to bed." He took my offered hand and led me into the last bedroom and shut the door. Inside, there were two full beds.

"You can have your own space if you want it." He gestured to the bed farthest from the door.

Before he even finished speaking, I was shaking my head. "I want to sleep with you."

He smiled and nodded like my decision made him happy. "Okay." For a long moment we just stared at each other, neither of us making a single move, then just like that night in my bedroom at Dasselaar's estate, which felt like forever ago but had really only been a little over a day, I threw myself into his arms.

Quin caught me, our mouths connecting in a punishing kiss that was full of desire and want, and colored with a subtle hint of fear. I knew what we were going to do tomorrow was dangerous, and if Dasselaar got his hands on me again, I wasn't going to make it out of the estate a second time, which meant I wanted this night with Quin, just in case it was my last. As my lips and tongue explored every inch of his, I prayed that one day we'd get to be together without the threat of being permanently separated looming over us.

For now, though, I would take everything I could get.

I clung to Quin like I would have clung to a thick branch in my chameleon form as he walked us into the bathroom and set me down on the edge of the counter while he reached into the shower and turned on the water. We were both still dressed in pieces of our tuxes from the gala since there had been no time to change, and Quin's fingers made quick work of the buttons, his warm, callused hands separating the fabric and pushing it off my shoulders. He trailed soft kisses along my collarbones as my fingers worked the buttons of his shirt open until I could press my palms flat against the honey-bronze expanse of his chest. He breathed in a ragged breath when my fingers skated over his nipples, and I saw his cock jump behind his zipper.

Carefully, he lifted me down off the vanity and slid the black belt of my tux through the loops with a whispered whoosh that made goose bumps erupt over my skin and my nipples pebble. He lowered to his knees until he was at eye level with my navel, and he kissed along the dark trail of hair that disappeared under my waistband. At some point, he'd worked my pants open and shoved them down my legs, but I'd been so distracted by his gentle touches that I hadn't even noticed until he tapped my ankle, encouraging me to lift it so he could remove my pants and underwear from around my feet.

My hard cock jutted out from my body, and Quin teased over the shaft with the same soft, reverent kisses he'd bestowed on the rest of my skin. The featherlight caresses of his lips were maddening even as I got drunk on them, my knees going weak as he stood and stepped back just enough to remove his pants.

We stood there, both naked, studying each other as though we'd never get the chance to do it again as the bathroom filled with steam. I noticed small imperfections in his skin that I'd left out of my drawings because I hadn't known they were there. Each freckle and small scar made him that much more real. He was no longer that stranger on the pages of my sketchbook, but a real live man I wanted to spend the rest of my life with.

Tentatively, my fingers connected the constellations of small freckles on his chest and traced the handful of scars along his sides, a longer one along his left hip, almost hidden in the vee of muscle at the bottom of his abs.

Quin shuddered as my fingers touched the silvery skin. "Appendix when I was twelve." He captured my questing fingers before I could respond and tugged me into the shower where he pushed me under the hot spray.

My muscles relaxed as the water sluiced over my skin, and I melted into Quin's touch as he washed my hair with shampoo that smelled like him. I returned the favor, switching places with him so he could rinse his hair. For a second, he turned his back to me, and when he pivoted again, I was on my knees, my mouth a breath away from his cock.

"Dimitri—" he started, but I cut him off.

"You got to taste me last time. It's my turn."

His growl reverberated off the tiles, muted by the running water as my lips closed around the head of his cock. I reveled in the heavy weight of him against my tongue and lapped at the salty precum that slipped from his slit. Rolling his balls in my palm, I let my fingers find the spot where I could massage his prostate from the outside and smiled around his length when I felt him tremble.

"Dimitri. God, your mouth." His hips stuttered forward, his cock brushing the back of my throat, and I swallowed around him, loving the possessive and primitive sounds that spilled from him. His hands tangled in my hair, and he used his grip to hold me still for a minute, my lips pressed tight against his body before he gently encouraged me to pull off and lifted me to my feet. "You were going to make me come."

I licked the taste of him from my lips. "That was kind of the point."

"I want to come inside you. Will you let me?"

"Yes. Fuck yes."

He reached outside the shower, a blast of cool air making me shiver until the door swung closed again. Quin had a little bottle clutched in his hand, and I knew this had been his plan all along.

"Turn around and bend over. Put your hands on the tiles."

His demand was no more than a whisper, but I immediately complied, presenting myself to him like I couldn't wait to feel him inside me.

Because I couldn't.

I needed it.

Craved it.

Slick fingers circled my hole and pressed inside. Quin's gentleness from earlier had vanished, replaced by possessive need as he worked me open with two fingers. I loved the stretch and burn and after so long without feeling someone else's touch, my body responded eagerly.

Or maybe that was just because it was Quin, my fated mate, who was touching me.

In minutes, I was rocking back against his hand, desperate for more, and Quin was quick to comply with my body's demands. His fingers were replaced by the thick head of his cock, and he slid home on the first thrust, impaling me on his length. The primal sound he made as my body engulfed him went straight to my core, making my balls tingle and wrapping around my heart.

Like this, there was no doubt Quin was mine, and I was his.

One of Quin's strong arms wrapped around my torso, hauling me up until my back was against his chest. In this position, Quin was so deep inside me he barely needed to move, pegging the spot that made my knees weak with every tiny thrust. His hand wrapped around my cock, and I looked down to watch as he jerked me with just the right amount of pressure, twisting his palm over the head on every stroke.

His mouth found the spot on my shoulder I wanted him to bite, and his teeth closed over the flesh in a teasing approximation of the real thing. A whimper shimmied its way up my chest, and Quin whispered a single word against the spot.

"Soon."

Then his mouth closed on the tendon again, and I came, my cock jerking in his grasp as I felt the hot rush of his cum deep inside me. Quin held me in his embrace until my body stopped shaking with aftershocks and his cock softened and slipped from my body. He washed his cum away and wordlessly cleaned the rest of my body, his gentle touches and caresses returning.

I loved the fact that Quin was tender and sweet yet primal and possessive, and as I fell asleep, warm and safe in his arms, I dreamed of getting to experience all the different aspects of him for the rest of my life.

CHAPTER TWENTY-THREE

QUIN

"WE'RE FIVE MINUTES OUT." Jack was driving one of the vans Reuben had rented back to Dasselaar's estate, and while we were on well-maintained roads, my stomach turned over and over like we were bouncing over rough terrain.

On one hand, I hated that Dimitri had insisted on coming with us, but on the other, I understood his need to see his sister safe. Nero had made one last-ditch effort to convince Dimitri that it would be better if he and I stayed behind, but the protest had fallen on deaf ears, both my mate's and mine. I wasn't letting my brothers go into the estate without me, and Dimitri would never let me go without him.

So here we were, both dressed all in black, on our way to rescue my mate's sister.

Jack took the turn that led onto the service road and swore. From here we could see the front drive where two black vans exactly like the one we were in were parked.

"I don't like this." Cal was leaning forward in his seat,

his eyes fixed on the vans in the front drive. "Someone else is here."

"I'm working on the feed. Give me a second." Felix's fingers flew over his laptop, then he too swore. "Fuck. It's Malveau."

"What is Malveau doing here?" Nero asked the question out loud, though we were all thinking it.

"I don't know. I can't get audio, but it looks like three of Dasselaar's men are down in the entryway and foyer." Felix clicked to another screen. "I'm looking for Dasselaar, but he's not one of the bodies."

Dimitri shuddered next to me but kept his jaw set.

"That might be good for us." Cal pulled out a gun and checked the magazine. "Maybe Malveau has taken out some of the trash for us."

Nero grunted, his uncertainty conveyed in the guttural noise.

Jack pulled the van to a stop in the alcove near the kitchen where Hadrian had hidden the car the night before. It was hard to believe it had been less than twenty-four hours since I'd led Dimitri out of the darkened estate.

Nero pulled open the door and we all climbed out of the van.

Cal held out his hand, and I passed him the gun he'd given me. He double-checked the magazine, nodded, and handed it back. "Shoot anything that moves, Quinny. No one inside is a friend."

"Except my sister." Dimitri's tone was tight, and standing as close as I was, I could feel him shaking. He had declined a weapon when Cal had offered because he didn't know how to shoot. Cal promised to fix that at the first opportunity once we were all back in Seattle.

"Yes, right. Except your sister. Nobody shoot the sister."

Jack and Nero nodded.

"Comms check." Felix's voice came through loud and clear and we took turns answering back. "Comms are good."

"Everybody know where they're going?" Jack asked, and we all responded in the affirmative. "Then let's move."

We followed on nearly silent feet as Jack led us to the concealed door and popped the lock. The hinges whined as the door swung open, and we silently walked inside. The pantry was a tight fit for all of us, but Jack found the door leading into the kitchen quickly and we spilled out into the empty space. Only the light over the large stainless steel sink was on, and the sun was hidden behind thick clouds so no light from outside penetrated through the windows.

Jack led the way through the kitchen and out into the hallway. From there, we diverged. Nero had the basement and old servants' quarters. Jack had the first floor, Cal the second, and Dimitri and I had the third.

Using the stairs we'd found the night we broke into Dasselaar's study, Dimitri and I climbed to the third floor.

"I've got Malveau." Jack's voice whispered over the comms. He must have moved closer because a second later, a smoothly accented voice spoke.

"Dasselaar, you know how much I hate to go back on a business arrangement, and when I shell out two hundred fifty-seven million dollars, I expect the merchandise I paid for to arrive as it should. So tell me, why was there no painting on the plane where it was to be delivered last night?"

Dasselaar sputtered, and Jack explained that one of Malveau's men had a gun on him. Dasselaar's voice shook when he responded. "I-I don't know. The painting left here as promised. It was delivered to the airstrip, to the plane you specified."

Malveau's voice rose in volume as he slammed his hand against something hard. "You lie! The case was empty except for the frame. Where is the painting?"

"I swear I don't know. I don't know. But I will find out. I'll find it."

Dimitri and I had tucked ourselves away in the alcove at the top of the third-floor stairs, listening as Dasselaar begged.

Malveau had had enough. "It is too late. Your little bait and switch has already cost me a lucrative client, and there is nothing I hate more than losing money. Kill him. Kill them all."

Rapid gunfire echoed through the comms and through the house so it felt like we were experiencing the assault in stereo. Moments later, the house went eerily quiet.

Dimitri and I stayed where we were, holding our breaths until Felix gave us the all clear.

"Malveau and the vans are gone. Jack, can you confirm Dasselaar is down?"

"Confirmed. I have two bear shifters and Dasselaar down in the study."

"Status update, everyone." Nero's voice was firm and commanding, and we all checked in.

"We're on the third floor." Dimitri and I left the alcove and started opening doors. "All clear so far."

"I could use a hand covering the first floor. Too many rooms." Jack sounded a little out of breath like he'd been running.

"I'm coming to you. Quin, can you cover the second floor?"

"Yes. We're almost done up here."

"Good." Nero swore. "I've got a lot of hidden rooms down here too. Felix, can you tell me where I'm at?"

Felix gave Nero directions as the rest of us continued searching for Athina. The last room left on the third floor was Dimitri's old room. He stood in front of it, staring.

"Are you okay?"

He nodded. "It couldn't be that easy, right? They wouldn't have put her in the same room where they put me, would they?"

"Only one way to find out."

Dimitri reached out and tried to turn the handle. "It's locked."

My heart rate picked up, wondering if that was a good sign. Since I'd picked the lock before, I made quick work of it this time, grabbing my gun from the waistband of my pants where I'd tucked it so I could have my hands free the second the lock clicked.

"Go ahead." I nodded toward the door, and Dimitri pushed it open while I covered him.

The room was empty, and I saw Dimitri's shoulders slump in defeat as I called the all clear for the third floor.

"Do you want to take anything with you?"

My mate shook his head. "You already rescued my

sketchbook, which was the only thing that mattered to me and was mine. The clothes were Dasselaar's. Little more than costumes to dress me up in when he needed me to be presentable."

"Okay."

Dimitri backed out of the room, leaving the door open, and we moved to the far end of the hall, to the back staircase to go down to the second floor.

"Ballrooms and this side of the house are clear. Quin, I'm coming to you."

"We're on the back stairs to the second floor now."

"Roger."

When we made it to the second-floor landing, I stopped. I heard someone down the hall on the front stairs. "Cal moves fast."

But it wasn't Cal I saw when we moved into the corridor, and I drew my gun, leveling it at the figure at the end of the hall.

"Dimitri!" Athina screamed and fought in Dasselaar's hold when she saw her brother, but Dasselaar, who was bleeding heavily from a gunshot wound in his shoulder, held her tighter and pressed the barrel of his gun harder against her head.

"I want my property back," Dasselaar snarled. He was looking at me, so I thought for a minute he was talking about Dimitri. "Where the fuck is the painting, Hunter?"

"Let her go, Dasselaar."

"Put your gun down and tell me where the fucking painting is."

"I don't have it."

Dasselaar scoffed. "Like hell. You think I let you into my

house because I wanted you here? I'm not that stupid. When one of Juno Hunter's grandsons appears on my doorstep at the exact same time the painting she spent her life looking for reappears, it was my only option for keeping an eye on you."

"Let Athina go and I'll tell you what I know."

With the way Dasselaar was holding Dimitri's sister, I couldn't get a clean shot without risking her, but I didn't lower my gun.

"No, I won't be doing that." His finger tightened on the trigger, and Dimitri gasped. Movement behind Dasselaar caught my eye, and I watched as Cal approached on silent feet, gun drawn and pointed at the back of Dasselaar's head. I stepped in front of Dimitri, trying to shield him from what I knew was about to happen.

"Don't you fucking move!" Dasselaar screamed, jerking Athina in his hold and making her cry out.

"The painting was a fake." I was trying to buy time for Cal to get set to take the shot.

"No, it wasn't. You saw. He proved it." He gestured with the gun at where Dimitri stood behind me.

"It was a fake. Dimitri is my fated mate. His animal form won't let him betray me, so he was able to make the painting seem like the real thing."

Dasselaar put the gun back to Athina's temple as tears ran down her face. "You're lying."

Cal was in position, and as he took aim, I turned and pulled Dimitri into me, hiding his face in my chest as the gunshot echoed around us.

"Dasselaar is down for good. Target is secure and unharmed." Cal helped Athina to her feet, and the second she was steady, Dimitri ran to her and wrapped her in a crushing embrace, both of them sobbing as they hugged.

Tucking the gun back into my waistband, I approached my twin and wrapped him in a hug of my own. "Thank you."

Cal shook his head against my cheek. "You're my other half, Quinny. I'll always have your back. Always."

His words healed something that had felt broken between us for a long time, and I held on to him a little tighter, feeling his love through our twin bond in a way I hadn't in a while. "I love you, Cal."

"Love you too."

We ended the hug with a back slap and stepped apart, Cal moving to corral Dimitri and Athina around Dasselaar's body while I discreetly wiped at my stinging eyes.

"Let's get the hell out of here." We hustled down the stairs and met up with Nero and Jack.

Jack pulled Cal into a headlock. "You always get to have all the fun, sweetheart."

Cal broke the hold and smacked a kiss on Jack's lips. "It's not my fault I'm the better shot."

"I wasn't even there to take a shot."

"But you could have been had it not taken you so damn long to clear your side of the house."

They dissolved into a steady stream of ridiculous banter as they walked ahead, leading us back to the kitchen.

Dimitri had his arm around Athina, but she turned to look at me. She was shorter than her brother by several inches, but she had the same glossy dark hair, wide brilliant green eyes, and flawless olive skin as her brother. Her features were a little finer, but like her brother, she was beautiful, even with bloodshot eyes now narrowed at me and tears still racing down her cheeks.

"Are you really Dima's fated mate?" Her question caught me off guard.

"Yes."

"Are you good enough for him?" She was little, but she was fierce, and I liked her immediately.

"Athina!" Dimitri hissed. "He just saved your life."

She shrugged like that information was inconsequential, her attention never leaving my face. "I asked you a question. Are you good enough for my brother?"

"I don't know, but I will try my best to be."

Her face split into a wide smile. "That is good enough for me." She held out her hand. "I am Athina Crysanthos. Thank you for saving my life."

I took her offered hand. "Quin Hunter, and my pleasure."

"Introductions later. We need to get out of here so Felix can wipe the security footage." Nero shoved us through the pantry door, and for the second time in as many days, Dimitri and I emerged through the hidden entrance and climbed into the waiting van.

CHAPTER
TWENTY-FOUR

DIMITRI

I'D NEVER FLOWN on a plane before, let alone a luxury private jet. When Athina and I had fled Cyprus, we'd bartered passage on a ship to Rome, then taken a train to Amsterdam. But now, having spent the better part of nine hours cocooned in the soft leather seat next to Quin, I could honestly say this was the only way to travel.

Athina had been without her medication since Dasselaar's men had taken her from the apartment, so she took a dose from the bag Quin and Hadrian had collected and promptly passed out. When she woke up a few hours later, Jack had handed her a pair of high-end, over-the-ear headphones and connected her to the onboard entertainment system. She'd been watching movies ever since, completely unconcerned that hours before she'd been held at gunpoint after being held hostage. I kept waiting for her to break down or go into shock, but it hadn't happened yet.

I was watching her when Felix dropped into the seat next to Quin and me and held out a navy blue folder. "Here."

"What is this?" I flipped the little booklet open to see my picture.

"It's a US passport. As soon as Quin told us about you, and later, your sister, I got to work on having them made. You have new birth certificates, social security numbers, and identities."

I studied the passport more closely. "Dimitri Hunter?"

Felix shrugged. "Seemed appropriate. I didn't want to change your first name, but Chrysanthos kind of stands out if anyone happens to be looking for you."

"How did you know my birthdate?"

Felix made a face at Quin. "Can you believe this guy? It's like he doesn't know how good I am."

"Yes, Felix. You are an amazing hacker and a genius." Quin rolled his eyes as he finished the statement.

"I know." He pretended to buff his nails on his shirt. "But in all seriousness, the old you no longer exists. I've wiped you from every public record, so there won't be any issue clearing customs when we get to the States."

I felt tears prickling the back of my eyes, but I blinked them away. "I don't know what to say. Thank you."

"Don't mention it. Julius also set you and Athina up with bank accounts. He can give you everything you need to access the funds as soon as we get to the house."

The tears that had threatened before slipped out now. "You didn't have to do that."

Felix put his hand on my thigh. "You're family now." He looked over his shoulder at my sister. "Both of you. And one thing I've learned about orca shifters is they are fiercely protective of their own."

I nodded because I couldn't get words out around the lump in my throat.

Felix started to stand, then sat back down. "Oh, one more thing. A doctor's appointment has been made for your sister for tomorrow afternoon. I did some research on the medication she's taking, and I think there are better options for treating her condition."

"We can't afford the more expensive options."

Felix smiled. "You can now."

The dam burst, and I turned my head, sobbing into Quin's shirt again as the roller coaster of emotions I'd been on for the last two days finally pulled into the station.

I was safe.

My sister was safe.

I'd met my fated mate.

And we were about to start a new life.

By the time we landed in Seattle, Quin's designer shirt was stained with my tears. Like Felix promised, Athina and I flew through customs with no incident and then we piled into a big black SUV with a Haida art orca decal on the back and were on our way to the Hunters' house.

Even though the air was cool outside, I opened the window and breathed in the unfamiliar scents of my new home. The ocean here was briny and the salty scent stuck in my nose. Pine was thick on the breeze, which also carried the faintest scent of coffee, and I loved it. I tried to focus on landmarks as we sped along the highway, but everything moved past in a green and blue blur.

The lights were on in the huge house when the SUV pulled to a stop. The house sat on an inlet, and in the distance, mountains stuck up out of the ground. Oddly, the view reminded me of Cyprus. While no one would say the Pacific Northwest and my homeland had the same climate, there were enough similarities in the landscape that I immediately felt at home.

Quin waited for me while I gaped at the huge house and the trees, and the water gently lapping at the rocky little beach beyond the backyard.

"Are you ready to go inside?" He placed a gentle hand on my arm, and I nodded.

Black and white tiles in the entryway gave way to warm hardwood floors leading into the rest of the house. The same honey-colored wood surrounded each door and window and featured on the wood and iron staircase that twisted up to the second floor. I'd barely stepped into the house, and it already took my breath away.

Somewhere deeper within the house, my sister laughed, and I almost wanted to cry again. It had been too long since I'd witnessed her joy.

"Are you hungry? Julius, Marcus, and Ben made lunch."

We'd left Amsterdam at nine in the morning, but it was just approaching noon in Seattle, and my body was confused. It should be dinner time. Regardless, I was starving, and my stomach rumbled as Quin led me into the kitchen.

Nero and Felix had disappeared to their room upstairs. Cal and Jack were at the table, both with large sandwiches and a pile of chips in front of them. I scanned the room for Athina and saw her through an arched doorway, sitting on a dark leather couch next to a man with light brown hair.

"Who's Ben?" I asked, doing a mental tally of all the members of Quin's family I'd met.

"That's me." The brown-haired man next to Athina turned around and then stood. He walked into the kitchen and held out a hand. "I'm mated to Hadrian."

"It's nice to meet you." I wished everyone was wearing a name tag so I'd be able to keep them all straight.

"You too. Your sister and I have been talking. I'm a professor at the University of Seattle. It's too late to get her into the art history program for this semester, but I'm going to see what I can do about getting her set up for the spring."

"Isn't that amazing, Dima?" Athina was on her feet too, bouncing on her toes with excitement.

"It is." Quin's hand found mine, like he could sense I was a little overwhelmed, and gave my fingers a squeeze. "That would be amazing, Ben."

"Don't mention it." He turned and sat back down on the couch, and Athina flopped down next to him.

Quin pushed me into a chair and placed a sandwich and chips in front of me. I ate on autopilot, listening to all the conversations around me. When I was done and had declined Quin's offer of seconds twice, I noticed the room had cleared out.

"Where did everyone go?"

"Cal and Jack are putting things away in the garage. Ben has an evening class to teach tonight so he left. Hadrian took him to campus, then went to check on his boat. Julius and Marcus, who I don't think you've met yet, are in the basement following a lead we got in Amsterdam. Felix and Nero haven't come down from upstairs yet, and Athina went to take a shower.

A shower sounded amazing, and I must have made a

noise because Quin grabbed my arm and started towing me toward the stairs, but I dug in my heels and Quin stopped.

"What's wrong?"

"Nothing. I want a shower, but there is something else I want more."

He cocked his head as if he were trying to figure it out before I told him. "What? I'll give you whatever you want."

"I want to see your orca form. Will you shift for me?"

Quin's eyes went wide. "Of course. Will you shift for me?"

I glanced at my feet before looking up at him again. "I'll try. I haven't taken my chameleon form in over a year, and I'm not sure how long it takes the antitransmutative drugs to get out of my system."

"It took three days for Felix to be able to shift after he was drugged, but I don't think Dasselaar had you on a very strong dose since he needed you to be able to access at least part of your chameleon side."

I hated that Dasselaar had taken the ability to shift away from me, but I was anxious to get reacquainted with that part of myself. "We'll see."

Quin changed direction, heading away from the front hall and the stairs and toward a set of warm wood and glass double doors that led out to a covered veranda and a deck. The new scents of home surrounded me when we got outside, and I stopped for a second, absorbing the simple luxury of being able to go where I wanted to when I wanted to. Having that freedom taken away had been a difficult adjustment, and I wondered if it would take me an equal amount of time to adjust to being independent again.

The air was a little chilly, but the sun was high overhead, and I tilted my face toward it and closed my eyes, letting the rays warm me through the slightly overcast sky. I hadn't put on shoes after I'd kicked mine off at the door, and the grass was cool under my feet. I was in borrowed clothes that were a little too big, but none of that mattered as I soaked up my surroundings.

Quin let me stay there for as long as I wanted. He didn't hurry me along or prompt me to try to shift. He let me take the time I needed, and when I opened my eyes, he was standing close, watching me.

"You look so content."

A small smile tugged my lips. "Because I am. I've never been here before, but it feels like this is home."

Quin's answering joy was almost palpable as he beamed at me.

"Can you shift out there?" I tilted my head toward the inlet. "You promised to show me."

"Yes, I can shift out there, but I want to see you shift first."

I closed my eyes again and slid into the part of myself where my chameleon form sat dormant. I focused on my limbs, on shrinking down into my much smaller form, but the transformation felt just out of reach.

Quin's fingers brushed over my skin. "Dimitri, your whole body is glowing. You're beautiful."

I pushed harder, trying to encourage the transformation, but still, it alluded me. I let go and opened my eyes. "I'm trying. I'm sorry."

Quin's expression was soft, and he reached out to caress my face, the rough pad of his thumb tracing along my cheekbone. "It's okay. We have all the time in the world."

He unbuttoned his shirt, and shrugged out of it, laying it neatly on a fallen log at the water's edge. "I'll go first." He winked at me over his shoulder and stepped out of his pants, which he also left neatly on the log. Then, naked, he waded out into the water as my mouth went dry. His ass was a thing of beauty, round and muscular, and if I thought it looked amazing encased in a pair of his designer pants, that was nothing compared to how it looked bathed in watery sunlight.

When the water reached his waist, he dove under, staying down for long enough that I started to worry before I remembered that he was an orca shifter and there was no possible way he could drown. Soon, a tall black dorsal fin broke the surface of the water, followed by the top of Quin's back. A puff of air and water was pushed out of his blowhole as he flicked his tail and glided toward me. My heart fluttered with excitement and the fear that only came from being so close to something so large and powerful. Quin turned in the water, and his saddle patch came into view, the thick brush stroke vee exactly the same as it was in his human form.

A tug deep inside me pulled a gasp from my lungs, and my mind fell into the place where my chameleon lived. This time when I tried to shift, the transition was seamless, my bones popping and shifting as they reformed, and I shrank in on myself until I was buried in my borrowed clothes. It took me a moment to figure out how to move in my fully shifted form again, but I finally got my legs under me.

Nosing my way out of the pile of clothes, I saw the world from a completely different vantage point. The expanse of the inlet was huge to me in this form, and if I thought Quin's orca was large while I was human, it was nothing compared to how it felt looking at him in the water while I was a chameleon.

He lifted his head and the warm iridescent glow that had been circling my hands whenever he was near shimmered around him. If I'd had any doubt he was my mate up until then, that doubt would have dissolved. Chameleon shifters only saw colors like that, a shiny mother-of-pearl aura, when we'd met our mates, and seeing it around Quin in his orca form confirmed everything I already knew.

He was mine.

I was his.

And we would belong to each other forever.

His dorsal fin disappeared under the water again, and when he emerged from the water next, he'd shifted back to human, water sliding down his chest as he ran toward me. He was out of breath as he knelt on the rocky shore and held out his hands so I could climb onto his palms.

"My god. Look at you." Quin's voice was thick with tears, and I was desperate to know what he was seeing. "You look just like me. Your coloring. It's exactly the same. And"—he let out a small strangled sob—"the saddle patch." He transferred me to one hand, holding me gently as his fingers traced over a spot on my back. His touch made my tail curl with happiness. "You are so beautiful, Dimitri, like this and as a human." He lifted me to his face and pressed his nose gently to mine. There was no way he could have known that was what chameleon shifters did to acknowledge our mates in our shifted forms, and it was just another way I knew that fate had picked Quin just for me.

He carefully set me down on the log next to his clothes

and lowered himself to sit next to me. I made myself comfortable, enjoying being shifted for the first time in so long, and Quin patiently kept me company until I was ready to shift back. I climbed off the log and pulled my human side forward, the stretch of my bones and skin unfamiliar after a year without fully shifting. The process felt like it took longer than it should have, but a handful of moments later, I was standing in front of Quin again on two human feet.

He wrapped me up in a tight embrace. "You are amazing. Gorgeous. So perfect."

"You are too. Can I swim with you sometime? I want to touch you in your orca form."

Quin's smile was radiant. "Yes. Anytime." Then he shook his head. "Except right now. There is something else I want to show you."

CHAPTER TWENTY-FIVE

QUIN

MY STUDIO WAS an old carriage house that my grandmother had never used. The forest had grown up around it, but she'd carved it out of the trees, refurbished it, and converted it into my sanctuary when I turned sixteen. I wanted to take Dimitri straight there, but neither of us had on shoes, and the smooth stones on the inlet's shore had been rough enough. The path to my studio was unpaved and littered with rocks, branches, and pine needles, so I rerouted us through the house so we could both put on shoes.

"Where are we going?" Dimitri put his hand on my chest to balance as he slid on his shoe, then bent over to tie it. We'd put our pants back on outside but not our shirts, and when Dimitri bent over, the too-big waist of his borrowed pants slipped down his hips. My fingers itched to strip them off him in the middle of the foyer, but I quelled the urge, knowing I would have him bare and under me almost as soon as I had him in my studio.

Then the only thing he'd be wearing was my claiming bite.

My cock thickened behind my zipper, and I adjusted myself while Dimitri wasn't looking.

Clearing my throat, I answered the question he'd asked. "You'll see when we get there. It's not far."

"Okay. I trust you." He put on his other shoe, and I ushered him out the front door. From where we stood just outside the front door, it was impossible to see the carriage house, and I took Dimitri's hand, twining our fingers together as I started down the wooded path that led to the place that felt the most like me.

The trees swallowed us up, hazy sunlight barely making its way through the thick branches as the sun hid behind a cloud.

"It's so quiet out here," Dimitri whispered.

"It is. I love living here. The city is right there—at night you can see the lights—but out here, it feels like a different world."

Dimitri made a small noise of agreement as we wound our way deeper into the trees. Before long, I tugged him off the main path, and down the smaller one that went up to the carriage house's front door.

"What's this?" My mate stared at the little building with wonder in his eyes, and seeing his expression made me light up inside.

Stepping up to the door, I tapped in my code. The lock clicked, and I pushed the door open wide. "Come in." The main light switch was right inside the door, and I hit it with my elbow, bathing the space in a warm yellow glow.

Dimitri gasped as he took in my space. While my room

at the house was immaculate, this space was not. A worn red couch was in the middle of the room in front of a gas fireplace, a soft, brightly colored afghan tossed haphazardly over the back, and several mismatched pillows piled in one corner from the last time I'd fallen asleep out here. Two old end tables sat on either side of the couch, paint rags and mason jars full of brushes covering the surface of each. The rug under the couch was one of my grandmother's castoffs that had been given new life in my studio a long time ago. It was now threadbare in places, but I refused to get rid of it. A dented apartment-sized refrigerator was backed up against the wall behind the couch, the handle mottled with multicolored handprints and fingerprints.

I walked deeper into the small house, and Dimitri followed until we were standing in the middle of my studio. The equipment set up along one wall made it look almost like a science lab, but that was where I mixed the pigment paints I needed to match old applications. I also used the equipment to produce my own pastels, though that was a medium I hadn't pursued in some time. I had several large easels in the space, each serving a different purpose. Two paint-splattered adjustable stools were shoved into a corner, and several industrial rolling storage carts with wooden tops were wedged in beside them, each overflowing with every supply I could possibly need. Some of the drawers were partially open and more rags hung from hooks on one side of the cart closest to where we stood. Canvases ready for paint were stacked against the opposite wall next to a large drying shelf, and completed works were in their own vertical rack.

A pottery wheel blocked the back door, and a hunk of

white marble with a half-carved bust was on a carving pedestal next to it, my chisels, rasps, and other tools laid out beside it.

An old golden yellow chaise had been shoved under the window, and that was where I wanted to lay Dimitri out and claim him as my own. I could already picture what he would look like spread out in my sacred space. The light in this section of the carriage house was harsher, brighter, and whiter, better for matching colors and the direction of brush strokes, but Dimitri didn't seem to mind as he took in my sanctuary with wide-eyed wonder.

He walked through my studio carefully like he was on hallowed ground and flipped through the completed paintings with reverent hands. When he got to the Lichtenstein I'd forged, the one that was about to be sent north to Jean-Paul Bouchard for his daughter's wedding, he held out his hand, his skin immediately changing to match the paint on the canvas.

His head swung to face me. "Is this real?"

I shook mine in answer.

"You did this?"

"I did."

"Quin, this is nearly perfect. I would never know I'm not looking at the original work. I'm not sure even an expert could tell the difference if the original was here and they were displayed side by side."

I shrugged. "I told you I was good."

"I've seen your forgery of *The Evolution of Man*. I should have known from that alone." He nodded at the painting he was still holding. "But this is beyond perfection. This is impeccable. It's a masterpiece."

"Thank you." I crossed the room and gently took his hands from the canvas, holding them in mine.

"You're welcome." He looked around the room before his eyes settled on mine. "Thank you for showing me this. You hide your artist's heart behind the designer labels and professional polish, but this"—he looked around again—"this is who you really are."

I should have known he would see my studio for exactly what it was, the truest expression of my soul, and I couldn't hold back any longer. Dimitri's understanding unlocked something primal, possessive, and needy deep in my core. He was mine, and I needed everyone who saw him to know it.

I had to see the proof of it on his skin.

"I need to be inside you, Dimitri. I need to claim you and make you mine. Here. Now. Please." The last word came out on a growl I couldn't contain.

"Yes." The word had barely passed his lips before my mouth closed over his and I lifted him into my arms, biting at his lips until they opened for me and my tongue slid inside. The first taste of him washed over me, and I wanted to devour him. He gave me back everything I was giving, his lips and teeth and tongue dueling with mine as he wrapped his legs tighter around me. I wasn't sure how we always ended up like this, with Dimitri in my arms, clinging to me like I was the only thing tethering him to reality, but I loved it. I loved holding him in my arms. I loved that he knew I was strong enough to hold him up in more ways than one.

His borrowed pants slid down his waist again as I carried him back to the chaise, and my palms connected with the smooth, bare flesh of his ass. I loved to touch Dimitri, and I'd become addicted to the electric arc of sensation that jolted through me when our bare skin brushed.

Hell, I'd become addicted to him.

And after tonight, I'd never give him up.

No one would ever take him from me because I would protect him with every cell in my body.

I tried to be gentle when I set him down on the chaise, but the huff of breath he let out told me I'd maybe been a little aggressive.

I started to say I was sorry, but Dimitri shook his head. "Don't apologize. Show me who you really are."

His words were my undoing, and I grabbed the bottle of lube I'd stashed in my pocket, hopeful this was where the day would take us, and shoved my pants down, kicking them and my shoes away.

Dimitri's eyes went wide as his hungry gaze slid over my body. He kicked off his shoes and unbuttoned his pants where they rested low on his hips. His green eyes sparkled like peridots in the bright overhead light, and his cheeks were flushed, his lips already swollen from my kisses. I loomed over him, my fingers finding the waistband of his pants and pulling them down and off in one fluid motion until he was bare beneath me.

His form begged to be carved or painted, to be captured forever so everyone could observe his beauty, and my fingers itched for a charcoal pencil and a sheaf of paper. Instead, I reached out, tracing my fingers along the lines of his arms, the contours of his chest, the muscles of his legs, committing each shadow and play of the light to memory in full color and branding every inch of him with my touch.

There was no part of Dimitri my fingers then my tongue and lips didn't find until he was whimpering and desperate beneath me, and every beat of my heart was etched with his name.

"Quin. Quin. Quin." My name fell from his lips like a chant, and I reached blindly for the lube where it had fallen next to him. The time for teasing was done. I slicked my cock and grabbed the back of his knees, pulling him up and almost off the couch as I lined up my cock and slid inside him, burying myself to the hilt on the first thrust.

A shudder raced down my spine as his body welcomed me home, his inner muscles clenching around me as he held me deep inside him.

This was where I belonged.

Dimitri was mine.

He rolled his hips, I snapped mine forward, and we found a rhythm that drove us both toward the edge hard and fast as our fingers scraped over flesh and our bodies slapped together, creating a symphony of erotic sound that echoed around us, our moans and cries of pleasure the chorus. When I'd imagined claiming my mate, my mind had always conjured images of careful plans, candles, Egyptian cotton, gentle lovemaking, and a civilized bite. But that was before I met Dimitri and realized my mate wouldn't just see the parts of me I put on display. He would see everything. And this, this primal rushed frenzy of lust and love, was so much better than I ever dreamed it would be. It was messy, and hungry, and loud, and perfect.

Dimitri gripped my arms, trying to pull me down to him, but with his legs over my arms, it was impossible. With our bodies still connected, I lifted him into my arms again, turned, and fell gracelessly onto the chaise, the worn chenille soft against my back and Dimitri hard and solid against my front. He pushed up, straddling me, and found an angle that made his eyes roll back in his head. His olive skin was flushed as I watched him ride me, my fingers pressing bruises into his hips.

But finger-shaped bruises weren't the only marks I wanted left on his skin, and I tugged him down, his breath stuttering in his chest as my lips and teeth found the spot at the base of his neck that would bear my mark forever.

"Do it. Quin, please. I'm yours." Dimitri's lips slid across my collarbone, his tongue dancing over the sensitive skin of my saddle patch.

My fingers bit deeper into the flesh at his hips as I called just enough of my orca side forward to elongate and sharpen my teeth. Dimitri trembled, and I knew he was doing the same. I let my teeth graze over the spot, then on a breath, I bit down, breaking the skin at the same time Dimitri's sharp chameleon teeth punctured my flesh.

For a second the world went white, then there was an explosion of color so bright it ripped my orgasm from me. I came deep inside Dimitri's body as I felt the hot rush of his release on my chest. Fully bonded, I felt Dimitri's orgasm like it was my own, pulsing through me on waves of color, neon and glowing, and lighting me up from the inside out until I felt like rainbows must have been shooting from my skin like light reflected through a prism. Through our new mate bond, I felt his joy, his contentment, and his love, and the words spilled from my lips.

"I love you, Dimitri. I will love you forever."

"I love you, Quin. I'm so glad you were the one to save me."

Dimitri settled his head on my chest as we basked in the afterglow and our new bond settled firmly into place. My cock softened and slid from his body, but neither of us made any move to get up or clean up.

We were just going to do this again.

And we did.

Until we fell asleep wrapped in the old afghan from the couch, Dimitri's fingers painting pictures in his cum on my abdomen.

I woke to sun streaming in through the windows, and rolled off the chaise slowly, trying not to disturb Dimitri. Wrapped in the fraying blanket, his face relaxed in sleep, he was heartbreakingly beautiful, and I needed to draw him exactly the way he was in that moment.

My favorite sketchbook and a drawing pencil were tucked away on top of one of my supply carts, and I grabbed them before settling on the floor next to the chaise and beginning to sketch.

The image came together quickly, the lines flowing from me, through the pencil and out onto the page.

Last night, Dimitri had said my forged Lichtenstein was a masterpiece, but as his form took shape on the page, I knew it was him who was the work of art.

"What are you doing?" Dimitri's voice was sleep-roughened as he blinked his eyes open and found me with my sketchbook perched on my knees.

"You took my breath away, and I had to draw you."

He sat up and held out his hand. "May I see?" I passed him the book and watched as his eyes filled with tears, a wave of happiness pulsing through our bond. "This is how you see me?"

I nodded.

"Quin, you've made me look beautiful."

Climbing to my feet, I settled next to him on the chaise and held his face in my hand, my gaze dropping to the shiny pink skin of my claiming bite before my eyes found and held his. "You are beautiful, Dimitri, and more precious to me than you will ever know."

A happy tear escaped from the corner of his eye. "I love you so much."

Our declarations dissolved into a passionate kiss that was well on its way to something more, when there was a knock on the door.

"Quin? Dimitri? Are you up?" It was Cal's voice on the other side of the door. "I know you guys claimed each other last night. For the record, I get it now, Quin."

"What do you want? We're a little busy. Newly mated. You know how it is." Dimitri giggled under me as I threw my twin's words back at him through the closed door.

"You need to get unbusy, and you probably need to shower. Marcus and Jules have info. We're all meeting for breakfast."

I dropped my head to my mate's chest, groaning while he laughed.

"We'll be right there."

My lips found Dimitri's again, and I pulled the afghan up over our heads, trying to keep our bubble of happiness intact for just a little bit longer while my twin continued to bang on the door like the annoying asshole that he was.

Dimitri laughed. "He's not going away is he?"

My sigh ruffled the dark hair that hung over Dimitri's forehead. "Not likely. No."

He pushed at my chest where I was pinning him to the chaise. "We should get up."

"No." I closed my mouth over the claiming mark on his neck, sucking hard, and he moaned, his cock twitching against my hip. "We should stay right here."

Cal's banging increased. "No fucking! Family meeting."

Dimitri giggled again. "Is he always like this?"

"Yes, and it's too late to turn back. You're mine forever now, so you're just going to have to figure out a way to deal with it."

He brushed our noses together. "I'd do anything for you."

"Including dealing with my pain-in-the-ass family?"

"Anything."

We caved to Cal's incessant knocking, slipping back into the house and up to my room, but we absolutely did not hurry through showering. By the time Dimitri emerged from the glass-walled enclosure, his knees were shaking and I'd added a bite mark to his ass.

When we finally made it downstairs, every member of my—our—family was crowded into the kitchen. Felix was perched on Nero's lap, scowling at his laptop that sat on the kitchen table while he nibbled a piece of bacon. Jack and Cal were sniping at each other under their breaths while exchanging a look that told me their banter was foreplay. Hadrian was reading a magazine. Ben and Athina were tucked into the corner, looking at something on Ben's laptop, which he was balancing between them, and Julius, Marcus, and Eli were deep in conversation near the coffee maker.

The room went quiet as every eye turned toward Dimitri and me as we walked into the room, then the silence broke into a cacophony of catcalls, wolf whistles, and cheers.

"Ignore them," I hissed to Dimitri under my breath as I pushed Julius away from the coffee maker and reached for a cup. "Coffee?" Dimitri nodded, and I filled the cup and passed it to him. "Cream and sugar are probably out somewhere since these heathens never put it away."

"I drink it black, but thank you."

I filled my own cup. "Me too." Knocking my mug against his, I settled myself against the counter by the sink and pulled Dimitri in tight next to me, then turned to face the room. "I thought we were having a meeting."

Nero cleared his throat. "We are, but I think congratulations are in order first." He lifted his coffee cup in a toast, and the room dissolved into cheers again, my stoic older brother leading the pack with a wide, knowing smile on his face. As quickly as he'd whipped them into a frenzy, he settled everyone back down with a sharp whistle. "Marcus, you said you had something to tell us?"

Felix raised his hand, bouncing a little in Nero's lap. "Actually, can I go first?"

"Sure, Lucky." Nero pressed a kiss to his mate's temple, and Felix beamed at him before pushing his glasses up his nose and turning to his laptop screen.

"So, our theory that the gala would bring out all the parties interested in the painting was one hundred percent correct. Since it was revealed that Malveau bought the painting there has been a ton of dark web activity focused on acquiring the painting. All through illegal channels."

Cal's brow creased. "But Malveau doesn't have the painting."

"Right. But it seems like only half the dark web knows that. The other half is looking for information about what happened to the painting after it left Dasselaar's estate. I'm keeping an eye on the speculation, and so far none of it is pointing to us."

Jack nodded. "That's good, then. We're in the clear."

Felix shook his head. "Not quite. There are a few people offering large sums of money for details about the painting."

"The kinds of offers that someone who'd just lost two hundred fifty-seven million would make in an effort to recover something they believe was stolen from them." Julius pushed off the wall and crossed to stand next to Felix so he could see over his shoulder.

"So, who is it?" Hadrian closed his magazine as he asked the question.

"We don't know. The posts are anonymous and the source is being bounced through a bunch of different IP addresses. I've been trying to isolate it, but so far I'm not having much success." Felix looked disappointed. "I think all the offers are coming from the same person, and given what I've been able to trace of their digital footprint so far, I think it's the same person who went looking for an accomplice inside the FBI before he stumbled upon Agent Cooper."

Nero gripped Felix a little tighter at the mention of the

dirty—and very dead, thanks to Cal and Jack—agent's name. "But you don't have any idea who it is?"

"Not yet." Marcus's low voice echoed through the room as he spoke for the first time. "But if we assume that whoever hired Malveau to buy the painting is the same person who turned Agent Cooper and sent him after Felix, then we have a lead."

Nero nodded for Marcus to continue.

"During the auction, Julius saw that as soon as the money left Malveau's account and Dasselaar confirmed receipt of the funds, a deposit in the exact same amount Malveau paid was deposited back into his account. That transaction was initiated by AB Holdings Limited. Jules sent me the details, and I found exactly what he had. The company is a shell corporation based in the Cayman Islands. So I kept digging. It took me a long damn time, but I was able to trace a transaction from Grove Core Industries into one of the shell accounts."

Nero's brow furrowed. "Why does that sound familiar?"

Felix tapped at his laptop and turned the screen Nero's way. "Grove Core is a global company specializing in sustainable, bamboo-based products, including furniture, textiles, biodegradable packaging, and construction materials. Their worldwide headquarters are in Shanghai, but they have offices around the world. Last year, the US CEO, Tessa Li, and her husband were killed in a car accident. The circumstances were suspicious and there was evidence of foul play, and while the investigation played out over months, no one was ever arrested or charged with a crime. Li's job and her two children went to her brother, Ethan Lin, who is the new US CEO."

"I know Ethan Lin." All eyes swung to Julius. "Well, not personally, but since Grove Core's US headquarters are here in Seattle, I did some digging into him for my, uh, little side project. He always seemed legit, working his way up through the ranks of the business started by his great-great-grandfather. As far as I could tell, there was no ill will when his sister got the CEO job. He'd been CFO for several years at that point, and by all accounts seemed content in that role."

"But since his sister died and Ethan was installed at the helm, the company has faced losses and their global stock price has fallen. He could be looking to acquire the painting so he can turn around and sell it as a way to give the company an infusion of cash." Marcus waved his hand from side to side like he thought that was an unlikely scenario. "Or he could be looking to use the painting to wash some of his money like we think Malveau was trying to do. Or there's a chance he has no idea money is being funneled out of his company to shell corporations that appear to be funding a search for the painting. I can only trace things so far without accessing the company's internal records, assuming anything relating to illegal dealings isn't immediately destroyed."

Felix shook his head. "I've come up empty so far too."

"Which means I'm up. If the company is starting to struggle, they'll be looking for some guaranteed, high ROI investments." Julius smiled a shark's smile like he smelled blood in the water. "Time for me to go hunting for a new client."

The ORCA series concludes with *Monochrome,* coming soon!
Preorder now: mybook.to/MCORCA4

After a career on Wall Street, Julius Hunter is content to live his life as a modern Robin Hood. Getting corrupt corporations to invest with him while he siphons their money into charitable organizations makes his blood pump, so when he's sent in to find out what the new CEO of a global company knows about money being used to fund the search for a priceless piece of artwork connected to his family, he's all in.

Ethan Lin never wanted to be CEO of the company his great-great-grandfather founded. He also never wanted to be a parent, but when his sister died in a car accident, he inherited her title and her two adorable children. Balancing life as the head of a corporation and as a new dad is a challenge, and with diminishing returns at home and in the boardroom something has to give.

When Julius shows up, offering help in both areas of Ethan's life, they learn they have more in common than they think. Including a shared enemy. Whoever is targeting the Hunter family also has their sights set on Ethan, and Julius will stop at nothing to make sure the man he's falling for and his children stay safe as the final pieces fall into place.

Monochrome is the final book in the Organization for the Return of Criminals and Assets (ORCA) series, featuring an orca shifter financier who had no idea he liked kids, a panda shifter hellbent on making sure his family's legacy doesn't end with him, and a final showdown that changes everything.

ALSO BY VINNI GEORGE

Contemporary Romance

Open Doors:

Hold the Door

Door Number Two

Revolving Door

Doors Open on the Left

A Foot in the Door

The Hidden Door

Open Doors: The Complete Series

Business as Usual:

The Time-Out

Standalone Shorts (Available to Read for FREE Through BookFunnel):

Story Hour

Shifter MPREG

Land and Sea:

Jonah and the Narwhal

Everett and the Wolf

Dominic and the Dolphin

Charlie and the Panther

Shifter Romantic Suspense (No MPREG)

ORCA:

Black & White

Grayscale

Full Color

Monochrome (Coming Summer 2025!)

ABOUT THE AUTHOR

Vinni George has been a lover of romance novels (of all shapes, sizes, and colors) since she first got her hands on one of her grandmother's Harlequins and has never looked back. She lives in Ohio with her two favorite guys (her husband and son) and, hopefully—one day—a dog. When she's not writing, Vinni can be found working for her family's business, which provides plenty of plot bunnies. In her spare time, Vinni is a soccer mom who dabbles in performance art, quilting, and various culinary pursuits and enjoys traveling.

Vinni's debut novel, *Hold the Door,* was a finalist and runner-up in Contemporary Gay Romance in the 2020-2021 Rainbow Awards.

Connect with Vinni:
Sign up for my newsletter at vinnigeorge.com.

facebook.com/vinnigeorgewrites
instagram.com/vinnigeorgewrites
amazon.com/author/vinnigeorgewrites
bookbub.com/authors/vinni-george

Printed in Dunstable, United Kingdom

63277916R00150